A World Beneath

Chapter 1

Brandon was sitting in the backseat of the rental car, playing Tetris on his Nintendo DS. Jack was next to him, furiously "slap-dancing" as the vehicle made its way down Route 50, a highway that stretched through the northern Nevada desert.   The boys' parents, Stan (a.k.a. Dad) and Holly (a.k.a. Mom), were looking for a sign that would tell them how many miles they were from their destination - Ely, Nevada.

Brandon taught Jack how to slap-dance about a year prior, and Jack was becoming quite adept at slapping his hands against one thigh, in an alternating fashion and bringing his hands together in a quick clapping motion before repeating the movements on his other leg. Back-and-forth he'd go, attempting to break some sort of speed record that didn't exist. His family was waiting for the final stanza but Jack's ambition was greater than their patience.

"How about you take a little break, Jack?" his father asked.

"But if I'm going to make the Olympic team ..." Jack started. Brandon looked up briefly from his video game to deliver a raised eyebrow and soft chuckle.

"You told him that slap-dancing's an Olympic sport?" Mom asked, looking directly at her elder son.

"Ya' never know, look at curling," Brandon responded slyly.

Mom offered a slight smile. "I think you can take a break without fear of not qualifying."

Jack laughed. He stopped and nudged his brother in the rib. Brandon didn't respond. He was too busy with his video game.

POP!!!

"Jack!" Mom exclaimed. "That's enough." She had a smile on her face but her tone was a bit more serious now.

"It wasn't me," Jack answered.

"The tire," Dad mumbled as he steered the car to the side of the dusty road.

It wasn't a great place to get a flat tire. You couldn't see anything except sand, the occasional cacti and some desert monoliths in the distance. The Lange family was on the last leg of their vacation adventure. The marvelous sights they had seen, the Grand Canyon, Yellowstone, and the Grand Titons, were fresh in their minds. The kids enjoyed the desert landscape, a little boredom notwithstanding, but were anxious to get to the motel so they could get something to eat and maybe watch some t.v. before going to bed. It wasn't late – about 5:00 p.m. – but they were all tired. They had been driving for about 6 hours, without any stops.

"Well, it's a good thing we have AAA." Mom offered after Dad confirmed that the rental vehicle didn't have a spare tire. Mom was a very pretty woman, about 40 years of age. She wore a purple short-sleeved top and capris, the perfect ensemble for a summer vacation through the western United States. She was the eternal optimist of the group and that would come in handy more than once on this trip.

"We're not getting much reception out here, but I think the call will go through." Dad said. The number for AAA was above the visor – one of the perks of having a rental car I guess.   Dad fumbled for the cell phone that was kept in the compartment just below the radio. He was about 43 years of age but often acted like one of the kids – except when he was tired. "You kids would be turning my hair gray, if I had any," he'd often say. It made the kids laugh and that was something that both parents were very good at doing. He wore a gray t-shirt that he purchased at Yellowstone which had a picture of a cartoon bear on it. The bear was spray painting an "X" over the words "Do not" on the "Do not feed the bears" sign. It was kind of corny, but so was Dad.

As Dad was talking to the AAA representative, Mom was trying to get the kids involved in an "I-Spy" game. It didn't take long for the game to take a turn for the laugh.

"I spy a giant butt!" Brandon yelled. Laughter filled the back seat. Brandon pointed to a large plateau in the distance, poking up into the red-tinged afternoon sky. He learned all about the landform from his fourth grade teacher and he never missed an opportunity to mispronounce the word, especially when Jack was around.

"It's pronounced 'b-yoot'," Mom corrected, rolling her eyes ever so slightly and shaking her head.

The boys laughed some more.

"I'm going to kick some b-yoots, if you're not quiet," Dad whispered as he held the cell phone to his ear and laid one hand across the mouthpiece.

Jack looked sheepishly at Brandon, who only made things worse by making a face like a dizzy pig.

Dad got out of the car, no doubt so that he could actually hear something other than his children's laughter. The wind kicked up the sand around the car and swirled around Dad's feet.

Mom gave up on her I-Spy game and picked up a cook book she had been reading at night, from the arm rest. The front cover read "100 Ways to Wing a Chicken" and it seemed to taunt the kids, as they both looked for something to snack on.

"It's going to be a while," Dad said as he returned to the driver seat. "They said they'll send someone out as soon as they can, but the local auto shop only has one tow truck and it's currently on another service call. I guess we should get comfortable. At least it's not too hot out." Dad's sense of humor was never lost on his family. It was about 95 degrees.

"Wait, what? It's not hot out??" Brandon challenged, taking a quick break from his search for food.

"Well, the sun should be setting soon. It'll actually get quite cool." Mom explained, still looking down at the book. Mom was great at multi-tasking.

Brandon found a couple of tootsie rolls in the bottom of a bag and handed one to Jack. He put a few others in his pants pocket. The minutes ticked by as the car's occupants tried to relax.

"Why did the car break down?" Mom riddled.

"Why?" Jack asked. His eyes opened wider in anticipation of some hilarious answer.

"It was 'exhausted'," Mom responded. She waited for the laughter and had to push Dad's arm a little to get the first chuckle. The kids soon followed suit.

"Are you sure it just wasn't 'tired'?" Dad quipped. The laughter continued.

"And what did it wear when it started to get cold," Jack asked.   "A muffler," he said impatiently, not even waiting for his family to respond.

"When is a car like a frog," Brandon asked, not wanting to be left out.

"When?" Everyone asked.
"When it's being toad," he blurted out, barely able to finish the sentence before leaning over in a heap of laughter. They all laughed and unofficially dubbed Brandon the winner, given the riddle's appropriateness considering their situation.

The wind whipped up and a horizontal wall of sandy magnificence engulfed the car.

Silliness abounds when the Sandman comes calling.

Chapter 2

Brandon and Jack had a fondness for the beach. They often visited the Jersey shore, mostly the Wildwoods, during their summer vacations. They were both good swimmers. Brandon was more of a daredevil when it came to jumping and riding the ocean waves. Jack preferred to explore the water's edge, where he'd find sea-shells and creatures that would inhabit his blue pail until it was time to go home. He created an underwater environment that enchanted him like nothing else.   He shared his findings with Mom and Dad and they enjoyed seeing his youthful enthusiasm and imagination on display.

"Wish we were in Wildwood," Brandon declared, wearing a well-worn navy blue t-shirt that read "Wildwood Crest, NJ" that he got on their last vacation at the Jersey shore. He pressed his nose against the window and gazed out onto a day that was almost over. The wind had settled down but left a sandy sheet across most of the road. One could barely make out the blacktop beneath. The desert fixtures were again visible, but like the setting sun's fiery sphere, they had taken their last look across the desert floor on this August day.

"I'm thirsty," Jack said. He reached into another bag on the floor and pulled out a half-full bottle of berry flavored water.   "Anyone want some?" Nobody did.

Dad glanced at his watch and looked at Mom. "Maybe I should call them again," he said.

With those words, the sun's rays made their final appearance and gave way to darkness.

Dad had been turning the car on and off in order to provide his family with the comforts of cool air from time to time, but he turned off the ignition as the heat had now dissipated. He tried calling AAA, but the signal must have been interrupted by something.

Jack finished his beverage, after spilling some on his white shirt and jeans. The spot on his shirt resembled a purple dinosaur eating blueberries. He began putting tiny pieces of a pretzel in the transparent container. He was naming each piece and imagining the rise of a new civilization. It reminded Brandon of the beach and the blue pail.

"I really wish I was in Wildwood," Brandon repeated. "I could go for a slice of pizza on the boardwalk, or maybe an ice cream." He watched the population explosion occurring in the water bottle.

"King Momo decrees that all wishes are granted to his loyal subjects." Jack had a good imagination and entertained his family with stories about lost worlds and adventure.

"All hail King *Moron*!" Brandon said.

"It's Momo," Jack countered. He shook the bottle a bit, no doubt re-positioning the King's soldiers in anticipation of an attack.

"Prepare for war King Moron!" Brandon declared. He attempted to swat at the tubular kingdom but forgot about his seatbelt, which was still fastened. The strap abruptly halted his advance on the Kingdom of Pretzalia. Jack maneuvered the bottle to his right side, to offer maximum protection. He picked up the tootsie roll wrapper that he had discarded earlier and balled it up.

"Catapults ready," he warned. He tossed the wrapper at the advancing horde that was his brother.

"Ahhhhh!! Retreat!!!" Brandon shouted. Mom and Dad looked at the two combatants and just grinned. They knew that even if Brandon appeared to be bullying Jack, he would often back down to let his youthful counterpart get the better of him. He was a kind and protective older brother.

The car began to rumble ever so slightly. Everyone looked outside, expecting to see a tractor trailer truck passing by. This had been a frequent occurrence during their 3-plus hour wait for the tow truck.

This time, they didn't spot anything on the road. The car continued to tremble as Mom and Dad looked around to see if they could uncover the mystery of the shaking auto. The seatbelts rattled against the sides of the car.

"Stan!?!" Mom uttered.

"I don't know," Dad answered. "It feels like an earthquake."

Now, that probably wasn't the best statement to make. With his family stuck out in the middle of nowhere and nothing in sight that would have offered sanctuary from a natural disaster, Dad's words only increased the kids' anxiety.

"An earthquake?" Jack asked.

"I'm sure it's nothing Jack," Mom managed, between throwing annoyed looks at her husband.

The car held together quite nicely, but its occupants felt a little queasy with each toss and turn. The wind seemed to pick up again and a wall of sand appeared on the horizon, just to the left of where the Langes were situated.

"Hold on everyone," Dad instructed as the wall got closer.

The trembling became violent shakes, like a giant child using the rental car as his personal snow globe. Soon, nothing was visible outside. The family instinctively ducked their heads as the sand struck the windows and windshield.

The good citizens of Pretzalia tumbled from their safe

confines onto the olive-green field that was the carpet beneath Jack's feet.

"King Momo!!"

Chapter 3

When the family awoke, they were met with the face of a man peering in the car's window on Mom's side. The visage was thin and pail. A gnarled toothpick seemed ensnared between yellowing teeth, perhaps trying to escape. The stranger wore a light gray jumpsuit, like the ones mechanics used to wear. It had a zipper down the front and patches on it that advertised various brands of gasoline and motor oil. The stains that covered the jumpsuit were dark and numerous and the garment hung from his shoulders like a wet towel on a hanger.   A filthy rag poked out of the chest pocket, dripping with grease, oil, or some other automotive liquid. Every so often, sand particles would blow onto the man and stick stubbornly to the dark oily spots.

"Well, hello," the man said. His voice was muffled as the car's windows were up and the vehicle was almost completely buried in sand. The only bare spot was the port hole that the stranger made.

The man was brushing the sand off of the car and he continued to do so, even as Dad attempted to get his door open. Dad pulled the handle and used his shoulder to push, but it didn't work.

"Just give me a second and I'll have you all out of there," the man instructed.

Dad shrugged. "I guess we can wait a couple more minutes, huh?" He tried to smile but it came out looking like he had just swallowed a fly.

After about 10 minutes, the family was able to exit the car. Brandon and Jack simultaneously shouted "Yay!" Brandon grabbed his DS, shoved it in his back pocket and proceeded to chase his brother around the car while Mom and Dad were still trying to get the feeling back in their legs. The sun was up again but it wasn't quite as hot as the previous day.

"Is everyone o.k.?" the man asked as he held out his hand for Dad to shake.

"I think so. Thanks. I'm Stan. This is my wife Holly, and our kids Brandon and Jack." Dad reached for the man's hand but pulled it back quickly as if he had just touched the hot coils on a stove.

"Sorry Stan. That happens every so often," the man explained with a grin.

Dad didn't know what to think. Mom was looking at him with a puzzled look on her face. By now, the kids had circled back to where their parents stood and were equally shocked by Dad's reaction.

Dad held out his hand in front of him. It was red and slightly blistered.

"Here, wrap it in this," the man instructed, pulling the dirty rag out of his pocket. Initially, Dad recoiled but before he could say anything, the dirty rag transformed into clean, almost pristine, white linen.

"How" is an old Indian greeting but the Langes used it in hopes of prompting a reasonable answer to the craziness that they had just witnessed.

"Don't be afraid," the man continued. He bowed at the waist and as he rose again his gray jumpsuit was magically transformed into a classic black suit, elegantly tailored to fit his now more robust body. Each of the Langes took one step back from where they stood and rubbed their eyes hard in hopes of waking from this obvious dream.

"Nope, that won't help, "the man indicated. "You are all very awake."

Dad whispered, "We're not in Kansas anymore."

"Thanks Toto," Mom responded quietly.

"My name is Cinder," the stranger said. He inhaled deeply, causing sand to fill his lungs. As he exhaled, a wisp of smoke billowed from the corners of his mouth and nostrils.

"Welcome to Zucarus."

"Thank you," Jack said. He had the water bottle again and held it tightly against his side. The Pretzalia townsfolk were nowhere to be seen.

Chapter 4

"Who are you? What are you?" Dad asked, questions that they all wanted answers to.

"My name is Cinder. I am the Great Fire Wizard, King of all that you see and don't see." The stranger had a sing-song way of speaking – almost like a child's nursery rhyme.

"This must be some sort of dream," Mom stated.

"That we're all having?" Dad wondered aloud.

"One of you has summoned my underling and I want to know why." Cinder demanded. "No one speaks the name of a Droplet without my approval." Cinder's face was charcoal black, with shades of white. He looked like a negative from one of those old cameras. When he spoke, his eyes reddened like sparkling rubies. He was an imposing figure, over 6 feet tall.

"Look. I'm guessing you're not from AAA, but we're really not sure what you're talking about," Dad explained.

"Silence!!!" Cinder demanded.

"Hey buddy, no one talks to my husband that way ... except maybe me." Mom scolded.

"Shhhhhhh," Cinder hissed, holding up a blackened finger to

his snake-like lips. His appearance was changing again. This time, the edges of his body seemed to fade into the background. His form became a mist that expanded into the now ashen sky. When the fog cleared, an enormous dragon with wings unfurled stood in front of them. It was a hideous beast with a comical flare. His underbelly was red and black like a checker board and his black wings were circus tents slightly tattered from years of use. Tiny flames flickered from his sinister mouth, ragged nostrils, and cavernous ears. Gray smoke engulfed him and made him look even more ominous.

"Tell me of The Speaker or I will set you all ablaze." Cinder's brow creased like a giant prune.

"We don't know what you want?" Dad yelled. "We don't know of a 'Speaker.'" The kids were now positioned behind Mom and Dad, as if their parental strength could protect them from the dragon's wrath.

Cinder took a deep breath and the Langes believed they had taken their last. They closed their eyes in hopes of avoiding the sight of the impending fire-ball.

But none came.

They opened their eyes and Cinder was standing before them, a smaller version of the dragon, in a silver and blue cloak. The flames were gone. The red eyes were softened to a pinkish hue, like those of the white rabbit, from Alice and Wonderland.

"Very well," he began, in an almost comical British accent. "If you won't tell me of the Speaker, then I will take you as my prisoners." He raised his arms, muscular limbs ending in six-digit talons, and spoke a few words that were inaudible to the Langes.

As if they were experiencing déjà vu, the ground began to tremble. But unlike before, when the massive wall of sand moved across the desert floor toward their location, the sand began to separate like a parting sea, walls gradually building on each side. Brandon covered his eyes with his arm and Jack did the same. Mom and Dad strained to see what was happening but the stinging wind was too much for their tired eyes.

The wind stopped.

Re-focusing on the separated sand, they could see a giant glass floor beneath their feet, as expansive as an icy lake. Monstrous mounds of sand bordered the crystal floor. Below it, they could see puffy clouds. Were they gazing into a giant mirror?   Doubtful, as they couldn't see their own reflections.

As Cinder moved his hand in an arc across the sky, the clouds were blown to the side.

"A city!" Jack cried out. Hundreds of feet below where they stood, the Langes could see what appeared to be a miniature land. There were buildings and bridges, and tiny things moving. Streams separated the buildings from expansive emerald fields and tree-tops. Although entranced by the beautiful view, the Langes were also immobilized by fear. It was as if they were floating in mid-air.

"Here," growled Cinder. "Let's get a better view." With that, the glass floor became a sheet of cellophane, crumpling under the family's weight. Dad, Mom, Brandon, and Jack plunged through the flimsy film. Down and down they fell, terrified of their likely fate. As the air rushed past them, they couldn't make a sound. Dad tried to call out to Mom, Jack to Brandon, but their voices were muted by some invisible force.

The four tumbled downward for what seemed like hours. Fear turned to curiosity as they didn't appear to be getting any closer to the earth below. And at the moment that each Lange wondered how this could be happening, a yellow light engulfed them and they found themselves standing on a cobblestone pathway, surrounded by large white marble columns and buildings reminiscent of the ancient Greek architectural marvels Brandon and Jack had read about in history books.

"Are we in heaven?" Jack asked.

"I don't think so, Honey," Mom responded, looking skyward to see Cinder flying through the clouds high above them, in his large dragon form. He demonstrated a delightful display of aerial acrobatics.

Brandon punched Jack in the arm. It was just a brotherly tap, maybe to calm him with a familiar action or to remind him that he still had an older brother who wouldn't let him get away with such silliness. Either way, Jack managed a slight smile.

It must have been "Zucarus". It was an awe-inspiring place. Butterflies flitted about beautiful gardens, filling the air with musical melodies that were generally reserved for the most gifted of songbirds. Streams of crystal clear water danced through the fields and composed their own bubbling ballads.   The sky was bright, not blue but a golden yellow. The air smelled sweet from the unique greenery surrounding them.   Tiny insects poked their heads up above the precisely manicured grass. The soil seemed to have a welcoming orange tinge to it.

"What kind of prison is this," Dad asked himself aloud, almost sarcastically.

"Don't be fooled by all of the pleasantries Stan," Cinder mused. "This is Benshar, part of Zurcarus. I can take it all away in a flap of a wing." As if on cue, the skies darkened, the flowers wilted, and the once pure streams slowed with the introduction of an oily sludge-like substance. The air smelled stale and the strengthening winds were frigid.

"Wasn't complaining, just asking," Dad muttered.

"You will remain here, in my splendid kingdom, until The Speaker is identified. It's up to you whether you experience the delights of my compassion or the misery of my impatience."

The lights went on again and the flowers returned. The Langes sat on a grassy plot of land next to the dazzling stream, pondering their predicament. They wondered who this "Speaker" was and how he might be able to influence the future of the Langes.

"Anyone have any idea who this Speaker is?" Dad questioned.

"No Dad," Brandon and Jack responded, almost simultaneously.

"I have no idea," Mom added.

"I'm hungry," Jack uttered, rubbing his belly in an effort to calm its rumblings.

"Well, let's have a look around. Maybe we can find something."   Dad offered.

The family found the cobblestone path again and began walking toward a large white structure. The butterflies followed them, singing their merry songs. A stream mirrored their movements on their left-hand side. Silver fish leapt from the waters and splashed the travelers with cool droplets. Dad made a lazy attempt to catch one, but they were too quick.

"*Be gone!*" came a soft, almost muffled voice from behind them, like someone was trying to talk underwater, or with a mouthful of food. The Langes looked around but couldn't find the source.

"Did you hear that?" Mom asked Dad.

Dad merely shrugged while Brandon and Jack continued to search their surroundings. The place was warm, almost tropical in climate.

"*Shoo*!!" it started again. The butterflies scattered.

"Is there someone there?" Dad demanded. By now, the Langes had stopped in their tracks. A family of grasshoppers stood still at their feet.

"*Those nasty little creatures ... always such a bother?*" the voice continued.

"Winnie the Pooh!" Jack exclaimed. Another punch from

Brandon followed.

"We can't see you. Would you show yourself?" Mom requested.

"Why, I'm right here. But I'll make it easier for you."

With that, a tiny drop of water shimmered on a blade of grass under the golden sky. The Langes all noticed it, and the fact that it was now growing in size, as other tiny water droplets from the stream seemed drawn to, and absorbed by the first.   More droplets marched in a procession that led to the growing original.

Soon, a tiny "water man" appeared at their feet, approximately one foot in height. He was in transparent liquid form, and one could make out features that resembled a small, elderly man.   With each movement, his form moved like soft Jell-O, or more appropriately a clear water balloon that was filled to its maximum capacity.

"Let us introduce ourselves," the tiny man started. *"We are Felix and the Southside Droplets."*

"Is that a music group from when you were kids," Brandon asked of his parents. They ignored him.

"Felix?" Dad asked. "Where are the others that you speak of?"

"We are all here." Felix explained. "As a Droplet, I would be too small for you to easily see. That is why I've asked some of my friends to join me, quite literally, for this conversation."

The Langes stood on their path, eyes opened wide, not believing what they were seeing and hearing.

"Droplets," Brandon asked. "That's what Cinder said. He said The Speaker called for one of you?"

"You are correct, young one." Felix said.

"Brandon. My name's Brandon. "Felix seemed to smile.

"I'm Jack," Jack said.   Felix nodded.

"Stan, and my wife Holly." Dad added.

"It is good to meet you all," Felix responded. With a squirt from this ear, or what appeared to be an ear, a spray of water bombarded an incoming butterfly. *"Get!!!"*

"Why don't you leave them alone? They're not hurting anyone," Mom demanded.

"Ahhhh.   They are spies of Cinder. They are called 'Flappers' and are mere tools of the Bad One, to listen in on our conversations and report back. Never say anything in front of them that you wouldn't want to say to Cinder himself." Felix

25

explained.

"Do you know why we're here?" Dad asked.

Felix began an exposition on the history and plight of the Droplets.

"*We were once a great collective, at home in a vast ocean,*" Felix began. "*Our world was home to the magnificent sea creatures and vegetation that inhabit other oceans and seas of your world.*"

"A collective," Jack interrupted.

"*Yes.   It took a centillion of Droplets to make up the Great Sea.   We lived in harmony with the sea life, the sun, the earth, until Cinder came and destroyed us. Using his fiery breath and magic, he caused all of the Droplets to scatter and remain separated in this world, hidden under a glass sky and a layer of course sand. "His magic keeps us apart, for most of the time, but sometimes, for a great cause, we can come together, at least in small volumes. One of you has called to our leader. And that is why we've gathered before you.*"

"Where are the rest of you then?" Brandon asked.

"*Scattered about this unusual kingdom,*" Felix resumed. "*Most are terrified and will no longer gather in large groups, for fear of Cinder's wrath. For if Cinder wishes, a Droplet may* become Steam.   Steam is forever enslaved as an evil minion of the dark Dragon. If he senses an uprising, he quells it with his scalding breath, until each rebellious Droplet becomes his vaporous Steam soldier."

"Then why risk that by talking to us," Dad asked.

"Because one of you is The Speaker, who holds the answers to our freedom," Felix reasoned.

"Momo's your leader, right?" Jack jumped in.

"Yes!!!" cried Felix.

Dad, Mom, and Brandon looked at Jack. Jack presented the water bottle that contained a few pretzel bits and an almost unnoticeable amount of water. Through it all, Jack was still holding firm to the plastic vessel.

"You still have that bottle, Jack?" Brandon quipped.

"And you must be The Speaker," Felix surmised, bending gently at the waste and bowing before the younger sibling. "It's an honor to meet you Mr. Speaker."

Jack bowed, awkwardly, and held the bottle out in front of him.   The muted rays from the hidden sun were enough to illuminate what must have been the last drop of liquid in the plastic container.

"And it is truly a pleasure and honor to finally meet you, Sir Moist." Felix continued, addressing the last drop of berry water in the bottle.

"He's kidding, right?" Brandon asked as he began the chuckling process. "Sir Moist?!?"

Now it was Jack's turn. He shoved his elbow into his brother's rib, not hard, but just enough to get his attention.

"The prophecy has come to pass," Felix declared. *"Four have fallen from the sky. It is time to prepare for war."*

"What, are we going to have a water balloon fight?" Brandon joked.

Another elbow to the ribs, and all was quiet, except for the flowing stream that seemed to dance with excitement, and the distant sound of songbirds.

Chapter 5

Jack was immersed in the story of the Droplets. Dad and Mom seemed less skeptical than Brandon.

"Am I the only one who thinks that we're either all crazy, or suffering from heat stroke?" Brandon asked.

"Look, I know it seems very irrational, everything that's happening, but what explanation can you offer?" Mom asked.   She hoped for a logical answer. "I don't think that we're all having the same dream."

"I think we should continue to look around, to see if there's a way back to sanity." Dad urged.

"But what about Felix and Sir Moist?" Jack questioned. The two had long since vanished into the nearby stream, without as much as a single instruction for the Langes.

"They'll be fine, and I'm sure they can contact us again if they want to," Mom said.

"But which way?" Brandon asked.

"How about that way," Mom offered, pointing down the path. A large mountain sat off in the distance. Patches of trees and vegetation lay at its feet.

"Good idea," Dad said. "That'll offer a good vantage point for viewing the rest of this strange world and maybe those trees or plants can offer something to eat."

They started off down the path. The sky dimmed and the stream that had welcomed the news of Sir Moist slowed. Fog rolled in from nowhere in particular.

"Oh no, I think it's back," Brandon warned. He pointed skyward to a dark figure that circled them like a hungry vulture.

"Quick, let's duck in here," Dad said. He motioned for Mom and the kids to enter the large white building that had been the focal point of their initial walk.

The building resembled the Parthenon. White columns held up a large triangular roof. The walls were made of speckled marble. A large wooden door was the only thing that stood between the slowly deteriorating outdoors and a hopeful sanctuary.

Dad turned the iron door knob and pushed with great effort. The door budged, but only a bit.

Cinder descended in a spiral pattern and called out to Jack.

"Speaker!!"   He hissed.

With the help of Mom and the kids, they managed to increase the space between the door and its frame. Inside, flickering lights seemed to welcome them.

"I think we'll be o.k. in here," Dad said, gently pushing his family into the grand entrance room, one by one. "Let's get this door closed." Again, they pushed with a combined might and barricaded themselves in with a wooden beam that they had found nearby.

A circular room presented itself with dragon-themed tapestries adorning the walls and a long oak table situated near its center. Dark wooden chairs surrounded the table, like trusted guards. The floor seemed to be made of some sort of heavy clay and each footstep taken was a bit of a chore until the visitors became accustomed to it. They explored the chamber and marveled at the sculptures aligning the base of the side walls. They were sculptures of strange creatures, not quite recognizable by the tourists.

Cinder's voice boomed outside. "Speaker! I've identified you and now you and your family are free to go." But the loud thud on the wooden door didn't instill a great deal of trust on the part of the Langes.

"I think we should stay here," Jack whispered.

Mom looked at Dad, and when another large thud interrupted their train of thought, they decided to remain indoors. They weren't sure whether they were safe from Cinder's presence but they were too tired care. While not comfortable, the chairs were put to good use. The Langes rested as the flickering candles from the chandeliers above badgered their weary eyes.   Soon, they were all fast asleep. Only Brandon dreamed – of the earlier conversations he and his family had with a miniature water man named Felix.

Though the magical nature of the building's walls prevented Cinder from entering (they had been built long ago by a prophet's sons), he had internal representatives who could carry out his bidding. The lights from above darted back and forth as they slept, recording their thoughts and visions.   Cinder had many spies, and the glowing Flares were among them. Ever vigilant, they instantly reported back to Cinder the goings-on within the chamber, including the dreams of a young boy.

Like a thought bubble appearing in the comic strips, Cinder could see the images that the Flares were projecting on a cloud over his head. The dragon soon learned about Mr. Speaker, Sir Moist and a Droplet plot. He wasn't very concerned because his formidable legion of Steam, Flares, and Others were historically successful at putting down insurrections. That is why his army of Steam was constantly growing, while the population of Droplets was dwindling.

But no human had ever entered his kingdom, and now

there were four of them. Cause for concern? He thought not. A reason to be wary? Perhaps. He had originally considered letting them go, but his ego preferred a different ending. Cinder ordered his Flares to lay siege to the Lange's temporary motel room. He figured it couldn't hurt to get rid of these trouble-makers.

Brandon was the first to awake, as wisps of smoke tickled his nose. He shook Jack into consciousness and both boys attempted to wake Mom and Dad. The Flares had taken over the long tables and were moving with surprising speed toward the chairs. Mom and Dad remained in a trance-like state. Sparks flew through the air like tiny orange ninjas, attacking the hair on Mom's head, and the back of Dad's shirt. The boys extinguished these small fires with furious and desperate slaps. The parents still slept, despite the boys physical and vocal pleas.

The floor became soaked from their perspiration. Shallow puddles soon formed beneath their feet, making their movements a bit more difficult. Sparks began to fly in their direction and thoughts of aiding their parents turned to self-preservation.

"Help! Help!" Jack cried out. He wasn't sure to whom.

The flames began engulfing the chairs but the intense heat did nothing to bother the slumbering couple who remained motionless in their seats.

"Let's get some water from the stream," Brandon suggested, pulling his brother toward the front door.

But no matter how hard they tried, they couldn't remove the large beam that blocked the door. It took four of them to put it in place and two of them wouldn't be able to lift it.

Hisssssssssssssssss.   A violent snake-like sound came from behind them, where their Mom and Dad sat.

They turned to face the serpent, only to find their parents sitting in a cloud of smoke. They were drenched, but otherwise none the worse for wear. They were slowly waking, as the curls of smoke carefully nudged them.

"*You're all safe*," declared a muffled voice from below one of the long tables. It sounded like Felix.

"Felix?" Jack asked.

"*No, not Felix,*" the voice continued. "*My name is Wheezer. I'm pleased to make your acquaintance.*" This being was similar in form to Felix, but he was much smaller. There were numerous, even smaller water formations standing in ranks behind him, but they didn't speak.

Wheezer explained that he came into being from the children's perspiration and his liquid army from the water molecules still present in the air. He didn't know anything of Cinder or The Flares, and had no recollection of the Droplets. He pointed out that his presence was merely the product of lucky coincidence and the boys' desperate and loving attempts to revive their parents.

"We are in your debt," Dad said graciously.

"Yes.　Thank you so much," Mom added.

With that, Wheezer sank to the floor like a snowman in a pizza oven. His soldiers followed suit.

Flares continued to dance from the light fixtures above but their movements were far less vigorous. They peered down at the family.

Brandon climbed up on a table and took off his shirt. He began waving it violently above his head, in a circular motion, like a helicopter.

"You know you won't take off, right?" Jack said.

"We have to put them out. There's no telling what they might do." Brandon countered. His efforts were in vain as the flames merely danced in mocking fashion at the boy's lack of height.

Mom and Dad pulled a tapestry from the wall. They joined their oldest on the table and began their attempts at extinguishing the candles. The flames were no longer mocking. The room was soon dark.

Chapter 6

They pulled open the wooden door and their eyes strained as the brightness of the outdoors flooded the room. They were still tired, but no one would sleep again until they could guarantee they'd be doing so in a safe haven.

Cinder was nowhere in sight, so they decided to continue their journey to the distant mountain. They were comforted by the fact that the familiar stream accompanied them on their journey.

"Thank you boys for your help earlier," Mom said, referring to their attempts at putting out the fire in the Great Chamber   (Jack has begun referring to everything as "Great" since Felix mentioned the "Great Collective" and the "Great Sea"). She held Dad's hand as they walked together down the cobblestone path. This is how the boys remembered them on vacations.

"No problem Mom. Seemed like we had some help," Jack stated.   Jack took things in stride, more than the rest of them. Perhaps it was because this "World Beneath" (as Brandon dubbed it) was simply a version of one of the worlds that his imagination might have created.

Every so often, Jack grabbed Brandon's shirt-tail. It was a comfort thing. He had left the water bottle upstream, and his brother was the closest thing to a security blanket that he had.   What a strange world they were in. If it wasn't for the existence of an evil dragon and a darker version of the kingdom, the Langes might have considered this a fairly successful vacation.

"Today's the day we were supposed to return the rental car. Boy, are they going to be angry." Dad mused.

"Do you suppose we should have gotten the Dragon insurance?" Mom laughed. Then, she swatted away another Flapper. They were all getting used to treating the beautiful fliers as pesky mosquitos.

It seemed like a long walk to the bottom of the Great Hill. The stream had taken a turn about a half mile back but the Langes continued on, hoping that the lush vegetation at the foot of the hill would provide them with at least a snack.

"We're almost to the Great Hill," Jack declared.

"Great! And maybe we'll find a Great Tree that bears a Great Coconut and we can have a Great Feast ...," Brandon teased.

"O.K., that's enough." Dad stated. Mom gave Brandon one of those looks that only a Mom can pull off.

Frustration had set in. They were all hungry. Their efforts weren't in vain though. They reached the edge of an overgrown orchard where flowering trees produced unusual fruit that looked like a cross between a grapefruit and a pineapple. Brandon guessed that Jack would call it the Great Fruit.

He was right.

Dad picked one off of the ground and opened it with one of the keys to the rental car. The pinkish orange skin was rather tough, but Dad was able to break through. Its inside resembled an orange, but there were tiny green seeds throughout.

"Well, I'll be the guinea pig," Dad suggested. He took a tiny bite of the exotic fruit, seeds and all.

When the rest of the family saw his frowning face and the puckered lips, they almost gave up all hope.

But then Dad smiled and said, "It's actually not bad." The fruit had a sweet taste, a cross between a banana and a pear. It had a gritty texture, but no one seemed to mind.

Dad plucked a few more from the tree and opened them up for Mom and the kids. They devoured several of them each, enjoying the unique taste that the Great Fruit had to offer. Maybe it wasn't their first choice, but it was better than tootsie rolls. After agreeing to continue with their trek to the top of the Great Hill, the Langes finished their "meal" and stuffed a few more pieces of fruit in their pockets for future meals.

The Great Hill had a steeper incline than originally thought. Clouds must have obscured the top portion of the jagged landscape. The Langes made a human chain, with Dad in front, followed by Mom, Brandon and Jack. The "engine," as Dad was spontaneously nicknamed pulled the passenger cars and the caboose up the slope, over some rocky terrain, and through some dense underbrush. Trees with sharp gnarly branches were scattered about, so their ascent was not direct. It took them several hours to navigate the challenging mountain side.

"We're almost there," Dad said. "It looks like there's some sort of cave over that way," he continued, pointing to a dark indentation on the Great Hill.

"First thing's first," Mom responded. "Let's see what we can see from the summit." Everyone was in agreement.

The "train" reached the Hill's peak. The group sat on the hard ground, to catch their breath, gazing out over a dark valley on the other side. In comparison with where they'd been, the other side of the Great Hill looked menacing. The land looked scorched, with gaseous pockets littering the blackened soil.   Molten lava flowed eerily amongst dead trees and rock.

Turning around, Mom, Dad, and Jack basked in the more

familiar land that they just traversed. Brandon's eyes remained fixed on the darker regions, searching for unseen monsters that might inhabit this new area. His objective now was to avoid a catastrophe like the one that almost cost him his family at the Great Hall. He didn't mind that Jack, and even his parents seemed oblivious to the obvious dangers facing them from the western portion of this new world.

"Jack, what's the most musical job on a train?" Brandon asked.

"What?" Jack asked, excitedly.

"The conductor." Both kids laughed. It brought back good memories. Every year, usually in November, they'd visit the train museum in Lancaster County and take a ride on the Strasburg Express for a scenic view of the local farmlands and countryside.

"Any ideas," Dad asked. Nothing from the top of Great Hill gave the Langes any clues as to a possible exit or escape.

"How about the cave?" Jack asked. Jack had an unknown tie to this world. His family seemed to know it.

"The cave it is." Dad responded.

"The Great Cave." Brandon stated.

Smiles all around.

Chapter 7

You might think it strange that the Lange family took a nonchalant attitude toward this World Beneath, not particularly shocked or fearful of things that were happening around them. That wasn't the case. Each member of the family had his or her own trepidations but Mom and Dad chose not to reveal theirs, to avoid scaring the kids any more than they already were.

As an eleven year old, Brandon had some of his own – monsters, demonic dragons, talking water drops.

Jack was in his own world – quite literally. This World Beneath was similar to places that usually resided in his imagination. He had been here before, if only in his mind, and he seemed to have a handle on things. It helped that Mom and Dad, along with big brother, were there to protect him, but in reality, maybe it was the other way around.

The sky never seemed to darken, except when Cinder made it so. On their trek to the Great Hill, it didn't happen once. Cinder's absence was curious. The Langes figured they were being watched but hoped that the Dragon King, or Fire Wizard, had other things on his mind – maybe the quelling of some insurrection plotted by a bucket filled with dishwater or a glass of iced tea. More likely, they were exactly where the Bad One wanted them to be.

They calculated that it was probably late evening in the real world, by the time they reached the cave. The sky above didn't signal that it was night time. There was no moon. There were no stars. The golden roof and an occasional passing cloud were the only visible things overhead.

The Langes were more careful and deliberate in their approach to the cave. Its darkness hid any clues to what might have been inside. As they ventured into the cave, it began to smell like sulfur. There were no signs of life, like bats, but they had an eerie suspicion that they were being watched.

A path led deep into the bowels of the cave and descended about fifty feet before ending at a rock wall. Dad used a tiny flashlight that was on the rental car keychain to help navigate the narrow passageways.

"Did we miss a turn?" Mom asked.
"I don't think so," Dad answered.

Jack reached out for the rocks in front of them. They were damp and slippery to the touch.

"Droplets!" he exclaimed.

He began searching for one of the water people, but there were no signs of anything except for the damp cave walls.

Dad felt the wall too, maybe in hopes of opening some magical portal to a more reasonable dimension. As he touched it, a small but steady stream of liquid flowed from the base of the wall. A terrible gurgling sound followed. The entire mountain seemed to tremble as the foursome were thrown to the floor.

A noise erupted from the entrance of the cave. It got steadily closer until the sounds of rock scraping upon rock forced the Langes to cover their ears.

"Let's get out of here," Dad urged.

But as they ran toward the cave's opening, it quickly became apparent that something was blocking their way. Mounds of rock and soil quickly filled the cavern and shook the Langes, quite literally, as their bodies were engulfed by a mixture of rock and debris.

Suddenly, they were thrust forward, in the direction of the cave's opening. They flew through the air, a stew of flesh, bone, dirt, rocks, and vegetation. But as they passed the entrance, their flight continued. The earth took them far out into the air, away from the mountain slope. The family and their earthen captor shot out into the open space, leaving the Langes lying on their backs on a long swatch of gray and brown soil that extended out like a plank on a pirate's ship, a good 80 yards from the mountain.

"Yuck!" came a booming voice from inside the cave. The voice was accompanied by a mixture of hot air and more debris. The Langes shielded themselves from the particles of dirt and stone that flew their way.

"You taste awful!" the voice continued.

With each word, the Langes could see the mouth of the cave opening and closing, ever so slightly.

About thirty feet above the entrance, two rock ledges seemed to separate from the rest of the mountain to reveal circular indentations, large craters that glowed setting sun red.

Could it be?

As they wondered, the ground they were standing on suddenly moved them closer to the mountain again, in a huge sweeping motion, like a dizzying carnival ride.

"Hmmm," the mountain spoke. "What food are you?"

The Langes were perched on the hand of a Zucarus Mesa Man. Its rocky digits carefully held the unlucky wanderers.

"We're not food," Dad responded.

"Nonsense! Every moving thing in Zucarus is food for the Mesa Men."

Most knew to stay far way from these veracious eaters, but strangers didn't have the luxury of such knowledge. The entire mountain shifted to the left, and then to the right. Then it rose, nearly touching the golden sky. The Langes elevated with it.

"We're not from this world," Mom explained.

"From where, then?" the Mountain boomed.

"Pennsylvania," Jack shouted.

"From where, then?" the Mountain echoed. It seemed to scratch its head with a set of petrified rock formations.

"The United States," Brandon offered.

"Hmmph," the mountain sighed. "I know of no such place." Even if he had been there, mountains have poor memories.

"What are you," Brandon asked.

"My name is Volcanius," the mountain thundered. "I am a Mesa Man."

Brandon introduced himself, and his family. "We are people, humans, and we don't want to hurt you." Mom put her hand on Brandon's shoulder in appreciation of his diplomatic efforts.
"Ha ha ha," Volcanius laughed. "I do not think that you

could hurt me, unless of course you get lodged in my throat again." The mouth of the cave stretched wide, as if Volcanius were grinning. The mountain sank slowly and sat in its previous spot. Small, almost bare trees were scattered amongst the rock formations like stubble of a man who hadn't shaved in a few days.

"I like you, Brandon. You are very funny," Volcanius continued. "It's not often that a Flapper or some other creature makes me laugh."

"Maybe because you want to eat them," Jack suggested.

"It's not that I *want* to eat them," Volcanius explained. "They just wander in, and get lost in my throat. It's lucky for you that you don't taste better."

"I have a riddle for you," Brandon said. "Who is a Mesa Man's favorite boxer?" Brandon asked, hoping to distract the humongous being from thoughts of eating his family.

"Boxer?" Volcanius responded.

"Sure. You know, a fighter or pugilist." Brandon urged.

"Then, I guess it would have to be Bellock" Volcanius responded.

"No, *Rocky* Marciano," Brandon replied, referring to the undefeated heavyweight who fought during the 1950s.

Mom and Dad were looking at each other, their eyes asking why their son was playing guessing games with a mountain. But their gaze was soon interrupted.

"I never heard of him," Volcanius groaned.

"Who's Bellock," Jack asked. No one seemed to hear.

"O.K., then what did one mountain say to the other mountain?" Brandon tried.

"What?" Volcanius asked.

"Let's meet in the valley." There was a long pause. Brandon thought he heard a cricket chirping in the distance.

Volcanius let out a huge guttural laugh. He shook and quaked.   Mountain streams were flowing down his rock face, as if he were crying with laughter.

After several minutes, the mountain was still.

"That was a good one, Mr. Brandon," Volcanius said. "Thank you for making me laugh."

"Who's Bellock?" Jack repeated. The Mesa Man looked down at the boy.

"Bellock? Why he is the greatest Mesa Man that this or any other land has ever seen. He's fought armies and wizards, giants and dragons. He defeated the Tarrons in the Great Mesa Wars. Bellock is a legend among mountains." Volcanius seemed to frown.

"What?" Jack asked, putting his hand on the large Mountain's arm.

"That was a long time ago. I have not seen my brother in many years," Volcanius explained. "Cinder and his darkest magic saw to it."

"That's too bad," Dad said impatiently. "Volcanius, do you know a way out of this world?"

"No.   This is my home. I seek no other." The Mesa Man said. "This wasn't always a dark place, you know?

"But, if you wanted to, is there a way out?" Dad persisted.

"Hmmmm," Volcanius pondered. Then he whispered, "I supposed if you defeated Cinder, the golden sky would open up and you could fly out of here."

Fly out of here. On the wings of a thousand Flappers? Dad shook his head. He wasn't convinced.

"O.K.   Volcanius. Do you know where we can find a Droplet named Momo?" Mom asked.

"King Momo!!" Volcanius exclaimed. The rugged grin

returned. "He dwells in the Lazi River. Maybe he can help you."

"Lazy River? Where do we get the inner tubes?" Brandon quipped.

"Pardon me?" Volcanius asked.

"Sorry, no Grey Poupon." Jack giggled.

The kids were at it again, but Mom and Dad hitched on to Volcanius' words.

"Where is the Lazi River, Volcanius?" Dad asked.

Volcanius lifted his large arm and pointed to the East, where the Langes had started their journey.

"Looks like we have another long walk guys," Dad said. "Volcanius, can we rest here before moving on?"

"Of course Mr. Stan," Volcanius responded. "You and your family are welcomed to stay for as long as you like."

With that, Volcanius showed the Langes a small ledge that sat just below his left shoulder. It was a spot that wasn't particularly comfortable, but it looked safe. A tiny stream trickled down from above, that offered a plentiful supply of drinking water.

The Langes slept, even with the snoring of the slumbering rock giant.

Chapter 8

"All hail King Momo!" exclaimed a muffled voice.

Jack was first to hear it and woke his family from their restful sleep.

"Five minutes more," Brandon requested. But Jack shook him awake, intent on his brother not missing anything.

The family sat on their perch, high above the grassy land below, listening to what seemed to be a fanfare of trumpets. They looked around but didn't see any royalty.

Volcanius was already awake. He had arranged a smooth path for King Momo and his court to traverse by leveling out some of the rocky terrain that led up to his formidable mouth.

"Below you, "Volcanius whispered, if you could call it that. The Langes peered down from their comfortable spot atop Volcanius' chest. Their rested eyes gazed down upon a band of sparkling water men.

The procession began with a plump Droplet, similar in appearance to a clear Michelin Man. He held a long staff in his liquid hand, and horn players followed close behind him. It was tough to determine whether there were five or six of them, as their transparent forms played tricks with the eye. Four other Droplets carried what appeared to be a wooden throne, upon which sat a splendid Droplet, dressed in a dashing suit reminiscent of days long past. The liquid garments hung loosely over the King's mighty form. Groups of soldier Droplets, about thirty in all, carried long spear-like weapons that glistened in the golden light.

At first it was difficult to see how large these creatures were, but their approach offered a surprising answer. Most were as large as a tall human. It became easier to identify their individual features as they progressed up Volcanius' belly toward his upper torso. Their faces could have been those of any ancient Spartan, or medieval knight.

The Langes watched in quiet amazement, sometimes shaken by Volcanius' sudden giggles that echoed throughout the valley below. He seemed to be enamored by the jubilant proceedings, like a child at his first parade. The procession soon reached the ledge where the family sat.

"Please stand," Volcanius instructed. The Langes rose to their feet. From behind one of the trumpeters, Felix stepped forward. The music stopped.

"Hi Felix!" Brandon shouted. The Mesa Man shushed the boy, and all was again quiet.

"By order of His Royal Dryness," Felix began, "it is declared that the four of you will serve in the Royal Wave." Felix appeared to be reading from some text that was written in invisible ink.

"Dryness," Dad questioned. "Isn't that a silly…" Volcanius shushed the elder Lange.

King Momo was off of his pedestal in an instant, followed by a smaller Droplet who resembled a young boy. The "boy" carried a large dropper filled with a multi-colored substance.

As he poked King Momo in the rib with the device, Felix explained to the Langes that the dropper was filled with sand from the various regions of Zucarus – red sand from the northern Sareen region, blue sand from Cobol in the east, green sand from western Annesia, and yellow sand from the south lands of Hessa.

With each pump of the dropper's bulb, beautiful swirls of multi-colored wonder were squirted into the King's form. The red and yellow sand mixed to color King Momo's flesh a reddish-orange, the blue and red converted his invisible robe into a splendid purple garment worthy of his position. The blue sand filled out his shoes and pants and a bit of green splashed onto his previously shiny dome.

"He's the only one of us with this power," Felix said. "That is why our King is sometimes referred to as His Dryness." The water absorbed into the sand as the last details were being put upon his new being. Bright yellow blots of sand became golden buttons that adorned the aqua-colored shirt that rested underneath his purple robe.

"I am pleased to meet your acquaintance," King Momo began, in a somewhat raspy voice, compared to the muffled voice of his First Assistant Felix. He sounded like an old blues singer from New Orleans.

"Bow, please," Felix instructed. Each of the mesmerized tourists took their bows. Mom and Dad nodded their heads, while the kids opted for the more dramatic bending at the waist.

"King Momo!" Jack declared.

"Jack!" the King responded.

Before anyone could say anything, Jack ran to the colorful figure. The two embraced like they were long-lost friends. The Langes merely looked at each other with shock.

"Do you two know each other?" Mom started.

As Jack peeled himself away from King Momo, remnants of sand littered his white t-shirt.

"This is the first time we've actually met," the King responded, "but we've seen each other often in Jack's imagination."

"And this world Jack, is this all part of your imagination?" Dad asked, wondering if they were all trapped in one of Jack's brain games.

"No, just King Momo. The rest of this is all new to me." Jack stated. He looked around at the King's court and they were now talking amongst themselves, their previous formality dissipating as the Langes addressed their king.

"Sir Moist!" Jack hollered.

"Good to see you Jack. It's General Moist now." The soldier held out a sword like weapon.

"Wow, congratulations," Jack gushed.

"Do you know of a way out of this place?" Dad asked the King.

"Only through the defeat of the Dragon Fire Wizard," King Momo answered. "With his fall, we'd all be free."

"Just as I said," Volcanius agreed.

"We'll be glad to help, any way we can," Dad offered. "Do you know why we're here?"

"One of you holds the key to his eternal power or certain destruction," King Momo said. The Langes looked at Jack. The Speaker was silent.

King Momo held out a sandy finger, pointing it in Brandon's direction. "He possesses the Light Box. With this device, we can all gain our independence. And rest assured we'll provide you with the support that you'll need."

They looked at Brandon, who sheepishly reached into his back pocket. He retrieved the video game system that he had almost forgotten about.

"Do you mean this?" Brandon asked.

With that, the Droplets, except for the king, fell down upon one knee. The mountain sagged around them. From the north and south, rumblings erupted as distant mountains slowly made their way to the meeting place - Bellock from the north and Terrock from the south joined their Mesa brother, kneeling before the Light Box.

"Wow, and I'm not even the high scorer," Brandon noted, a bit sarcastically. He actually was.

"Welcome brothers," Volcanius said to his mountain kin. "It's good to see you again."

Something big was happening (no pun intended). The Mesa Men had been separated for a hundred or more years, punished by Cinder for their previous insolence. Bellock was bigger than Volcanius, broad and gray with bulging rocks emphasizing his massive arms and torso. Very little vegetation dotted his form.

Terrock on the other hand, the youngest of the three, was a large green, plant-, tree-, and moss-covered variation of his brothers. He was smaller than both, with smoother edges.

They once made up a very large mountain chain that stretched for nearly seventy-five miles – the Great Ridge. birds, mountain goats, pumas, and other creatures inhabited them (creatures once snatched by Cinder from the topside world because they were thought to be The Speaker).

When the Mountains resisted Cinder's efforts to establish a dark colony of Steam Soldiers in their region, he destroyed most of the ridge and banished two of the Mesa Men to distant reaches of his dismal dominion. Only Volcanius remained in his original spot, at the edge of the Steam Soldiers' encampment. He was the barrier between that which was still good in Zucarus and the rotten spoils that Cinder and his sinister army left after the demolition of the Great Ridge and surrounding western region.

And now, out of a sense of revived hope, or just desperation, the three mountains were together again, if only figuratively.

Chapter 9

"You're much bigger now, Felix," Brandon said to the Lange's first Droplet friend.

"Yes, you'll notice that we're all bigger than the Droplet figure that you initially met," Felix agreed. "We are the Droplet leaders. We must be fearless and strong, for those who are too afraid to fight. Maybe through our strength and determination, they will find the courage to join us."

"It looks like you have some strong allies in the Mesa Men," Dad said.

"Indeed," stated King Momo. "Volcanius, Bellock, and Terrock are each powerful associates.

Terrock was a majestic ray of light and life. His mere presence could disrupt the grumpiest of foes. His brothers often envied the ease at which he could turn the mood of those around him.

The king explained how Bellock was the middle mountain, and was a proficient fighter. His boulder fists could easily crumple the most hardened enemy.

Volcanius, the oldest and more modest of the three, was perhaps the most powerful. He could project molten lava from his pores when enraged. Unfortunately, Cinder sometimes used this power to his own advantage.

"They will serve us for the purposes of defeating the Steam Soldiers and the Others," King Momo continued.

"Who are the Others?" Jack asked, vaguely recalling the details that King Momo spoke of, perhaps from a long-ago dream.

"The Others are the miscellaneous creatures that serve Cinder," King Momo stated. "They include the Flappers, Flares, and Mole Rats. And we will need you and your brother in order to defeat Cinder and all of his evil cohorts."

"Brandon and Jack?" Dad and Mom asked simultaneously. They clutched their children to their sides and held them tight.

"Of course," King Momo continued. "Only they have the requisite size to fit through the tunnels, and the necessary power to defeat Cinder."

The parents' jaws dropped. Everything was quiet and still. The kids thought they heard another cricket and imagined tumbleweed blowing by them.

"We're not going to let our children fight that beast," Mom declared.

"If you need soldiers, I'm willing to enlist, but the boys must be protected," Dad argued.

"Perhaps you can help us with the Steam Army, but Cinder can only be defeated by the Speaker and Light Box Carrier." King Momo was adamant in his assessment of things.

"If he thinks we can do it, maybe we can." Jack said bravely. "Anything to get back home." His bottom lip quivered a bit as he thought about the evil dragon.

"You're just kids," Mom countered. "You're *our* kids and we're not going to let you do something so dangerous."

"It's our job to protect you," Dad added, patting Jack on the top of his head.

"If they don't defeat Cinder," said King Momo, "there will be no protection for any of us. We will surely perish. I will not force the children to fight, but I ask that you discuss this as a family."

With that, all but one of the Droplet soldiers disappeared into the mountain, regiment line by regiment line behind the King. The echoes of tiny splashes could be heard by all. General Moist carried the large dropper to where his king stood. He gently squeezed the bulb and then inserted the clear tube into King Momo's left arm. With the release of the bulb, the colorful particles of sand were almost instantly sucked back into the clear tube. The colors merged into a brown, sandy color.

"We will await your answer," General Moist said. "Please consider everything that you've heard, and everything that you've seen in Zucarus since you've arrived. And remember that even the tiniest of stones cast into the water can make enduring ripples."

General Moist walked away and faded into the distant slope of Terrock, dropper and all.

Mom and Dad were left to ponder the words of the militant water man.

"Nothing seems real in this place," Dad started. "But we've all experienced pain, fear, and almost every emotion known. It all feels real, but as intelligent beings, we know that this is just a figment of our imaginations."

"But if we can imagine all of this, can't we imagine victory against Cinder," Brandon answered. His sudden seriousness surprised his parents. They looked at him with a sense of wonderment and pride.

"You think that you and Jack can really do this?" Mom wondered aloud.

"We can, Mom." Jack stated. His lip no longer quivered. He had a steely resolve that made Mom and Dad wonder who the adults were in this familial group.

"If you're going to do this, we have to make smart choices," Dad explained. "We need to learn about our enemy and prepare for what will come."

"I can help you with that," Volcanius interrupted. "There is someone who can tell us all about Cinder."

"Who?" Brandon asked.

"His name is JayJay," Volcanius answered. "He's a Flapper."

"I thought Flappers were Cinder's spies," Dad challenged.

"Not this one," Volcanius stated. He opened his mouth wide and pointed to the back of his throat with his gigantic rock finger. "I have him trapped."

"I thought you said that you ate all the creatures that wandered into your cave?" Jack asked.

"That is true, for the most part," Volcanius responded, "but I thought this one might come in handy at some point. In order to defeat your enemy, it's important to know your enemy. And who better to sing his song than a Flapper. I've hidden him away in a deep corner of my left lung."

"How do we get to him?" Brandon asked.

"It will be a rather long journey, but I can give you directions if you'd like," Volcanius offered. He began drawing them a map on the side of his torso, with a sharpened rock. It would read as graffiti to the unknowing, but would give the Langes a precise path to JayJay.

"Wow, that looks like a very long way," Jack noted.

"We'll be with you the entire time, Honey," Mom mentioned.

"Oh, I'm sorry," Volcanius said, "The passage ways will be too narrow for you or Stan to navigate. The children will have to go alone."

"Those aren't the tunnels that King Momo mentioned, are they?" Mom asked, biting her lip in anticipation of the answer.

"Not exactly," Volcanius responded. "As long as they stick to the path, they won't have any problems."

"And how are they supposed to communicate with JayJay once they meet up with him?" Dad asked. "Flappers just sing like birds, right?

"Very good question," Volcanius rumbled. "That's why they won't be going alone."

Volcanius shrugged his right shoulder and the mountain

shook. A white bird fluttered down from above and landed at Brandon's feet. He looked a bit like a seagull, but smaller. It made the boys homesick for their favorite summer vacation destination. But unlike the sea birds, this one had a marvelous red plumage sprouting from its head.

"His name is Greely," Volcanius said, introducing the family to his feathery friend.

"Well howdy, folks," the bird sang with a perfectly stereotypical southern drawl.

"Hi," Dad said, surprised by the accent.

"Hello," Greely said, now without even a hint of an accent. The bird was adept at changing his speech patterns and now mimicked Dad's east coast accent.
"You're cool," Jack stated emphatically. He loved the way that the bird spoke, with a steady cadence and the confidence of a king.

"Why thank you," Greely responded in a child-like voice, his cheeks turning a pinkish hue.

"Does anyone speak any other language?" Volcanius asked. "I'll show you what Greely can do."

"I know a little French," Brandon joked. "Bonjour."

"Bonjour mon ami [Hello my friend]," the creature said in a

perfect French accent. " Je m' appelle Greely   [My name is Greely].   C'est un plaisir de vous rencontrer   [It's a pleasure to meet you]."

"Wow, that's incredible," Dad marveled.

"He can speak with any creature and understand their language." Volcanius explained. "And he can also determine whether someone is speaking the truth.

"atsthay eryvay unnyfay [That's very funny]," Brandon spoke in Pig Latin.

"Otnay asay unnyfay asay ouryay acefay   [Not as funny as your face]," Greely joked back. The bird smiled warmly.

The boys laughed and their parents enjoyed every minute of it.

Chapter 10

"I gathered some supplies for you," Volcanius said, addressing Brandon and Jack as they began preparations for their trek into the deep recesses of the mountain's chest. "Look on that ledge over there," he continued, pointing to a flat surface, about 50 feet from where the boys stood.

When the boys reached the ledge, they found Jack's old water bottle, left for him by King Momo. They also saw Dad's flashlight, some Great Fruit, and a large branch that was carved into the shape of a sword. Brandon quickly grabbed the weapon while Jack was left with the more mundane items. Mom and Dad were busy a few yards below, examining the map that Volcanius had drawn. Not wanting the kids to get lost, Dad took a receipt from his pocket, one from the rental car place, and they used it as their canvas. Mom carefully copied the map using a nearby stick and some red clay that she had found on a nearby rock formation. The kids returned to their parents with their stash of goods. "Here," Mom said. "Dad and I drew you a map. It's not perfect, but it should help."

"Aw, Mom," Brandon sighed. "I've memorized the map. We'll be o.k."

"Nonetheless, you're taking the map," Dad instructed,

stuffing the tiny piece of paper into Jacks pocket. "Don't lose it."

"On the back, I wrote down a few questions that you can ask JayJay," Mom continued. "Try to get as much information about Cinder as possible, but be careful."

"But won't he be coming back out with us?" Jack asked. "Can't you ask him yourselves?"

"Oh no," Volcanius replied. "If he escapes his present prison, he'll surely fly away."

Greely watched as the family said their goodbyes. When he sensed they were finished, he swooped down and landed on Brandon's left shoulder.

"I will watch over them," Greely promised, in a booming voice. He must have been hanging out with Volcanius.

"Thank you," Mom said.

The trio climbed up to Volcanius' lower lip. Brandon and Jack looked down at their parents a few times and took comfort in their calm demeanor.

"See you soon!" Dad yelled, as the kids and their newfound pet made their way into Volcanius' mouth.

"They'll be o.k.," Dad said, putting his arm around Mom.

"I know." Mom stated.

"I just wish I had something warmer for them to wear. It can get cold in caves."

"I'll keep them warm," Volcanius said, moving his mouth ever so slightly so as not to crush the Lange boys and their faithful sidekick.

The boys ventured deep into the dark cave. The metallic flashlight provided just enough light to allow Jack to read the map. Brandon said they didn't need it, but there were at least a couple of occasions where they were happy to have it. Brandon used the wooden sword to feel around in front of them, to avoid any sudden walls or drops. Every so often, they'd hear Volcanius moan in pain, as Brandon accidentally poked him in his throat.

"Sorry," would be Brandon's reply.

As they progressed through the mountain, the damp walls that they experienced earlier gave way to drier, warmer walls.

"I thought caves were supposed to be cold," Jack said.

"I know," Brandon responded, "It's pretty hot in here."

"That's because I'm a volcano," Volcanius' booming voice explained.

Although they were shaken each time Volcanius uttered a word, the boys didn't mind. It was as if they had a fourth party on their expedition.

"We figured," Brandon replied, "but I thought you were dormant."

"I'm calm on the surface but lava boils like blood through my veins." Volcanius noted. "That's why you must stay on course. A diversion down the wrong path can lead you to a pool of molten fire."

"You must get awful heartburn," Brandon joked. He almost regretted saying it, as Volcanius' easy laugh caused a mini-earthquake and the explorers had to hold on for their lives.

"Stop with the jokes," Jack warned. "All of these rumblings are going to make me sick."

"Can I have some water?" Brandon asked. Jack readily handed the bottle to his brother, who took a couple of sips, making sure to save plenty for his companions and their return trip.

The hours went by. To pass the time, Brandon would make up riddles for Jack and Greely. He made sure to whisper the answer so that Volcanius wouldn't burst into laughter.

"How did the scientist know that the earthquake would be

bigger than the last one?" Brandon asked.

"How?" Jack and Greely whispered.

"Because he was a 'Size-mologist'," Brandon replied. The giggles were muffled by hands and a wing, because they knew that laughter was contagious. Sometimes Volcanius asked them to speak up, but the boys kept quiet as their uneasiness grew with each step closer to the Mesa Man's lung.

Soon, they no longer needed the map, as they followed the sounds of a meadow-lark imitator for the last hundred yards of their journey. It was extremely dark and the flashlight dimmed to a faint hue as the batteries slowly drained.

Reaching a dead-end, the explorers searched the black chamber for the singing butterfly.

"JayJay?   Are you here," Jack started.

"Seeeeee-ooo," the flute-like melody responded. "Seeeeeee –yeeeeeer"

"Over here," Greely commented. The boys followed their friend's voice and made their way over to the far wall of the discovered room. They strained to see the Flapper. The light from the flashlight made everything look yellow, but one could make out various shadings on the fluttering wings of this 5-inch creature.

"*Who are you?*" JayJay asked, translated by Greely.

"We are the Threatening Three," Greely answered, before Jack or Brandon could utter a sound.

"*Please don't hurt me,*" JayJay pleaded. He flapped about, and made circular and figure-eight patterns through the air, but made no effort to flee. The time it took Greely to translate JayJay's words was minimal, but the process was a bit confusing to the boys at first.

"Answer our questions, and we will let you live," Greely demanded. He then whispered to Jack to read the questions that his Mom had written down on the back of the receipt.

Jack fumbled for the paper, still enamored by the curious creature that hovered near his head.

"Number one," Jack started, straining to see the written words.

"You don't have to be so formal, or have you been drinking too much water" Brandon insisted, "No bathroom around here - just read the question."

Jack punched Brandon in the arm.

"You're next, if you don't answer the question," Greely threatened, hoping to further intimidate JayJay and spare Jack and Brandon the embarrassment that comes with exposing their silly youthfulness. JayJay darted this way and that way, seemingly confined in an invisible box created by his own fear.

"Where can we find Cinder?" Jack asked, in the sternest voice he could muster. He was taking his cue from Greely, who clearly knew how to handle Flappers.

"No! No!   You mustn't ask me questions about him?" JayJay screeched, his wings flapping like a hummingbird's.

"Don't tell us no!" Brandon hollered. He raised his wooden sword as if he intended to strike the frightened creature.

"Stop!" Jack demanded. He stepped between his brother and JayJay.

"No, Jack" Greely growled. "If JayJay is too afraid to speak, we will release him from his fear."

"But, it's not right," The Speaker pleaded. He glanced at Brandon and caught a glimpse of a wink. He quickly realized that this was just part of the plans. His brother wouldn't really strike down an innocent.

"O.K.   Maybe you're right. If JayJay doesn't want to talk, let's stuff pebbles in his mouth and pluck his wings," Jack offered, giving a couple of winks to his fellow threateners.

Brandon lowered his sword. Greely sat motionless, perched on top of Brandon's head and their mouths hung open like miniature caves. They looked at Jack, flabbergasted by the young boy's wicked suggestion. Jack realized that he might have gone a bit overboard with his words.

"Or maybe," Jack continued, "we can just continue to talk harshly to him."

Brandon rolled his eyes and if a gull could have done the same, it would have.

Chapter 11

"Where is Cinder?" Brandon demanded, shining his light into JayJay's eyes. Brandon took over after Jack's schizophrenic attempts at interrogation. It was probably the tenth time he had asked the same question.

"*Noooooooooooooo!*" JayJay cried.

This was getting them nowhere. Jack took out the water bottle and unscrewed the top.

"*Nooooooooooo!*" JayJay repeated. The nearly undetectable eyes of the Flapper grew to the size of dimes. "*Not the Droplets!!!!!!!!!!!*"

Hmmmm, the Threatening Three looked at each other and smiled.

"Answer the questions or I'll introduce you to a bottleful of Droplets." Jack said. His technique seemed to be working this time.

"*O.K. O.K.*" JayJay consented. "*I'll tell you. But please don't tell Cinder.*"

"Cinder will never know," Jack promised. Brandon nodded his head.

"*Cinder lives deep in the bowels of Volcanius,*" JayJay said, "*in*

a chamber protected by his Elite Steam Battalion, or ESB."
The Three looked at each other, trying to hide their fear.
They imagined the Dark Dragon just below where they
stood, slowly making his way through the mountain toward
their location.

"Does he know that we're here?" Brandon asked.

"*Not unless you release me and allow me to return to his
side,*" JayJay replied. "*But that doesn't seem to be in the
cards, right?*"   Jack smiled. He was beginning to like this
little stool pigeon.

"Why did he capture me and my family?" Brandon asked,
proceeding to question two of four.

"*The prophecy explains of his destruction, caused by The
Speaker and Light Box Carrier,*" JayJay indicated. "*And I'm
guessing that I am speaking to them right now. Am I right?*"

"Maybe," Brandon replied. "Tell me how Cinder can be
destroyed."

"*I do not believe that he can. He is too powerful,*" JayJay said.

Jack looked at Brandon, his confidence dwindling a bit.

"But if someone wanted to stop Cinder, how could it be
done?" Brandon requested.

"Just ask him to stop," JayJay said. *"And maybe he'll stop just long enough to explain how he's going to rid this world of the likes of you."* JayJay seemed to have a new found courage. Brandon was discouraged.

"There must be a way to take away Cinder's powers," Greely said.

"I know of none." JayJay countered. *"Why don't you tell them about the prophecy?"*

"Because we're looking for an alternate method," Greely explained.

"Maybe you should tell us about the prophecy," Brandon suggested.

"No. We must find another way," Greely insisted.

"But what could it hurt, just to hear ..." Jack began. Greely held up his wing, like a traffic cop halting traffic.

"Very well," Greely conceded. "The sky will open. Four will fall. A Speaker will inspire. The Carrier will challenge the Great Fire Wizard. The sky will burst. Evil will fall. Good will fall."

"The good will fall?" Jack managed, his lip beginning to quiver again. Brandon put his arm around him.

"Yes." Greely confessed. "That is the prophecy. For ages, we've been told the story of the Four and the Battle that ends in their fall.

"But the bad will fall too," Brandon offered.

"Yes," Greely agreed. "That is the prophecy."

"Do you have any more details?" Brandon asked. "Maybe we can change the part about the good falling."

"The stories are vague." Greely replied. "There are many variations to the stories but they're pure speculation.

"I don't believe in that nonsense," JayJay said. *"Cinder won't fall.   Cinder will rise. I've seen it in my dreams."*

"You don't know anything," Greely said, glaring at the brainwashed aerialist. He actually sensed that the Flapper was telling the truth.

"If I don't know anything, why did you come to seek answers from me," JayJay asked.

"Tell them how to avoid sneak attacks by Cinder and how they can safely infiltrate his underground lair," Greely appealed. "I know that somewhere beneath those delicate wings, a true heart beats for the days before Cinder."

"As dark and dreary as this mountain prison is," JayJay

began, *"it's a haven from the constant demands of the Dark One. I do have visions of a past life. But they quickly fade with memories of my more recent occupation as Cinder's spy."*

"You can redeem yourself, your reputation," Brandon offered. JayJay pondered the boy's statement and welcomed the glimmer of hope.

"Seek shelter when the lights dim," JayJay said. *"Cinder's presence is always preceded by a darkness, and a rotten odor that is initially very faint. Pay attention to these signs, because they will signify his coming, be it in wizard or dragon form."*

"Thank you," jack said asked. The Flapper's tiny mouth moved ever so slightly into an upward arc.

"... and to get into Cinder's chamber, undetected?" Greely asked.

"It's impossible," JayJay sighed. *"There's the ESB, hundreds of my brethren, regular Steam guards and the Rats that protect his inner sanctum. Even if you managed to defeat them, this would give Cinder enough warning to plot an easy escape."*

"Not defeat them," Greely corrected. "Is there a way around these guards?"

"As you know bird, the Steam guards are invisible," JayJay

said. *"There's no mist or fog, because water molecules no longer exist in their bodies. They are gaseous survivalists. How could you hide from that which cannot be seen?"*

"Can we bribe them?" Jack asked.

"With what?" JayJay responded. *"There's no good left in these beings. They aim to serve evil. There's nothing that you have that could satisfy their appetite."*

All seemed lost. But then Brandon had an idea.

"Are there lights in Cinder's lair?" Brandon asked. He knew that whether you're visible or invisible, darkness did not discriminate.

"There are some torches and the glow from an underground lava flow," JayJay recalled.

"What if we turn out the lights so that the only thing that can be seen is darkness?" Brandon asked.

"That's brilliant," Greely explained.

"Yes, but remember that Cinder could easily turn on the lights with a simple fiery breath," JayJay reported.

"Then we'll need a back-up plan," Jack said.

"JayJay, how close are you with some of the Flappers that

guard Cinder's dwelling?" Brandon asked. "Would they listen to you?"

"I have many friends, but most wouldn't risk the wrath of their master for even their best buddy," JayJay replied.

"What if you convinced them that the prophecy was right, that good and evil would both fall? Would they still follow an evil ruler who was destined for annihilation?" Brandon quizzed.

"I don't know," JayJay admitted. *"Maybe I could get some on our side. But if the prophecy is true, then why would you bother to fight when an inevitable end awaits all of us."*

"Because maybe we can change it," Brandon suggested. "I have to protect my brother, my family. I HAVE TO TRY." A tear streamed down his face, hidden in the darkness.

They were all touched by Brandon's devotion to hope and family. They each quietly pondered their expected fate but daydreamed about possible alternate outcomes.

"We will try," Greely promised. "And I'm speaking for two."

JayJay nodded. He stopped flapping his wings and gently floated onto Jack's shoulder.

As the four headed back to Volcanius' mouth and Mom and Dad, a boy's tear lay silent on the cavern floor. It wasn't absorbed into the warm ground. It didn't evaporate from the heat rising from the lava flows below.   It sat there, stubborn and proud, perhaps engineering its own last stand or dreaming of a heavenly reunion with its brothers and sisters.

Chapter 12

As the kids and their flying friends headed back, Volcanius began speaking again.

"What are you doing with JayJay?" he asked. "Don't let him out!"

"It's o.k.," Jack said, "he's with us."

"You can't trust him," Volcanius warned. He was doing his best to shake JayJay off of Jack's shoulder.

"Yes, we can," Greely reassured him. "It seems he's had a genuine change of heart." Knowing Greely as an aviary lie detector, he was encouraged by his friend's pronouncement of JayJay's moral enlightenment.

"Volcanius, why didn't you tell us that the tunnels that King Momo spoke of, and Cinder's lair, lay beneath you?" Brandon asked.

"I thought that you'd no longer be friends with me," the Mesa Man told them. "You see, Cinder confiscated the land beneath me. My lava protects him from outsiders, and in a way, my body is his castle wall. I've tried moving but my feet are forever entrenched in the earth beneath me."

"Well, friends don't lie to each other," Brandon remarked, "so from now on, nothing but the truth, o.k.?"

"You have my word," Volcanius promised.

The four found Brandon's and Jack's parents eagerly awaiting their return. The couple greeted their children with hugs, kisses, and verbal accolades for a successful journey. But the joyous mood turned sour when Mom noticed the Flapper sitting on Jack's shoulder.

She attempted to swat at it, but Jack quickly dodged the blow.

"It's o.k. Mom," Jack explained. "This is JayJay. He's one of the good guys now."

"Are you sure?" Dad asked.

"Uh huh," Volcanius confirmed. "He's on our side."

Jack told his parents all about the journey and the information gathered about Cinder, his whereabouts, the prophecy, and Brandon's plans for successfully destroying the Great Fire Wizard.

"But if the prophecy is true ..." Mom began.

"We can change it Mom," Jack stated.

"Or, if we can't, we can at least insure that the evil is destroyed and no other creature gets trapped in this world," Brandon proclaimed.

"That's very noble, son, but there has to be another way," Dad said.

"I have some ideas," Brandon announced.

For the next ten hours, the Langes began formulating plans for their next steps. Volcanius was in on it, presenting the family with his version of the strategy that King Momo and his allies would use to disrupt the actions of Cinder's armies.

Essentially, the boys would make their way through the tunnels to Cinder's lair. Greely and JayJay would accompany them. Greely would translate for JayJay, to give the boys tips as they approached Cinder's lair. JayJay would also act as ambassador once they met up with the other Flappers.

King Momo, the Mesa Men, and Mom and Dad would attack the Steam Soldier encampment so that Cinder's nearby guards could not be fortified further by additional reinforcements.

Then, the challenge would come. Brandon and Jack weren't sure how this would work, but they had to find something that would take the dragon out of its element.

Cinder came around every so often during their planning sessions. But with the advanced warning system that JayJay had told them about, Brandon and Jack were able to get everyone into the cave just in time to avoid his attack. Each time, Volcanius would close his mouth ever so gently to offer his guests maximum protection.

When an occasional Flapper would try to eavesdrop on their conversations. JayJay or Greely would either chase them off or attempt to persuade them to join the cause. It generally ended in a chase.

"Do we know when the King and his men will be returning?" Dad asked Volcanius.

"When you are ready, I will put out the word," Volcanius said.

Mom and Dad weren't quite sure how Brandon and Jack fit into all of this but their confidence grew with the successful retrieval of JayJay and their detailing of plans to find Cinder. They were ready but stalled a bit before letting Volcanius know, wanting some more alone time with their kids before the war began.

"What's the first thing you're going to do when you get home?" Jack asked Brandon.

"Order out for a pizza," Brandon replied.

"Yeah, with pepperoni," Dad added.

"And mushrooms," Mom requested.

"Ewwwww, No mushrooms!!" the boys protested, rolling around on the ground and holding their stomachs.

They all laughed.

How could these kids fight a dragon? How could they save a kingdom, practically by themselves?

"Do you think you're ready?" Dad asked. The laughter stopped and things became serious again.

"I think so," Brandon replied.

Dad began removing his wristwatch. It had a black leather band and a dark blue New York Yankees insignia on its face. He had had it for as long as Brandon could remember. He wore it to the first game he and Mom took Brandon to, before Jack was born.

"Here. Take this." Dad instructed. "Mom has one too." He pointed to her Nightmare Before Christmas timekeeper.

"Thanks," Brandon said. He knew that this was a big deal. Dad wouldn't give up his Yankees watch to just anyone.

"Take good care of it, and yourselves," Mom pleaded.

"All of our efforts will have to be coordinated and precise,"

Dad continued. "Though we're not going to be with you in the tunnels, the actions that we'll take will be for your protection. Both of you know your strengths, so use them."

Brandon and Jack nodded.

"Let's get some sleep," Dad urged, looking down at his wrist out of habit.

"10:15," Brandon said.

"It's past your bedtimes," Mom responded.

"Aww Mom," Jack whined.

"We're gonna need to be fresh," Brandon reminded him.

The family slept on a bed of moss, just below Volcanius' chin. The others watched over them as they slept. Drops of water from Jack's water bottle broke free of their plastic container and formed a Droplet soldier that stood guard. This allowed Greely and JayJay a moment to rest.

All was calm before the storm.

Chapter 13

They awoke to the sound of trumpets. Surrounding their position were hundreds of Droplet soldiers, standing at attention.

Jack peered down the mountain. He had actually been up for a few hours, very nervous about what was to come.

Regiment after regiment of water soldiers carpeted the mountainside. Armed with spears, swords, and other unique weapons each stood erect, shifting ever so slightly with each breath of wind. Their equipment wasn't liquid-based items but tools made of wood and metal. They swished around in each soldier's fluid grasp, like a mischievous child's finger through a glob of melting whipped cream.

King Momo, Felix, and General Moist stood to the left of where the Langes had been sleeping. His Dryness was not in his colorful wardrobe, but mirrored the image of the General's troops in their watery form. This was serious.

The fanfare continued for several minutes.

"You ready, Jack?" Brandon asked.

"Yes. Are you?" Jack responded.

"Sure. " Brandon confirmed.

When the music stopped, the King, Felix and General Moist sought counsel with the Langes.

The entire group reviewed the battle strategy and plans for attack. Mom, Dad and the boys were sworn into "The Wave," the name of the Droplet Army, while Greely and JayJay were dubbed Defenders of the kingdom in a less formal ceremony.

Then King Momo addressed all of those who were present, using a megaphone to cast his voice over the entire area. His scouts were alert in case Cinder or some Flappers chose to attend this invitation-only affair.

"I want to thank all of you for coming here today," King Momo began, taking turns looking at each group of allies – Mom and Dad, The Speaker, the Light Box Carrier, Felix, General Moist, the troops, the Mesa Men, and finally Greely and JayJay. "This is a good day to be good."

"The land is now dry, except for a few pools where the fish and aquatic creatures reside," he continued. "The horizons are flat, except for where we stand. And beneath us are hordes of terrible beings, no doubt making preparation for defense against us."

The Langes looked at each other. The kids had Flappers in their bellies. Wasn't the attack going to be a surprise?

"Sure, they know that we are coming. How could they not notice the physical changes to this land? They know of the prophecy and what surely must come. But they could never foretell the specifics of our intended action, the depth of our commitment to this cause, or the extent of bravery that pervade this mountain today."

"Let them see us coming," the king allowed. "Let them see the multitudes of good that will stand against the Steam Soldiers. Let them see the innocent children who will lead us to victory, and their flying assistants who will help them on their journey."

"Speaker," King Momo summoned, "Please grace us with some words of wisdom and hope, as those before you have come together in harmony to fight in your honor." He whispered something in Jack's ear.

"Ummm," Jack started, "What letter of the alphabet always wins?"

The soldiers broke ranks to look at each other, but no words were uttered.

"Victor-E," Jack said.

"All Hail The Speaker!!" came the call from the mountain side.

"Oh brother," Brandon mumbled. "That was not one of your better ones." But, Brandon thought, perhaps Jack's role in all of this was to inspire with humor. Maybe that's why Cinder wanted to identify him and destroy him.

The boys were called over to a smaller group of strategists – Dad, Mom, Felix, and General Moist.

"At 12:00, we will increase our attacks in the West and initiate the northern advance," General Moist said. "If you get to Cinder's lair before then, find a place to hide and wait until 12:00 before proceeding. We're hoping that our attack in the West will prompt some of the Steam Soldiers to leave Cinder's lair to fight us."

"How will we know that they've left if they're invisible," Jack asked.

"According to Volcanius, you will hear a loud whistling sound, like steam leaving a teapot," Mom explained.

"And these masks, which will allow you to breath despite the toxins around you, might offer some visual confirmation as well," Felix offered, handing them to the boys.

"Mom's not going to fight too, is she?"   Brandon asked.

"In a way, yes." Felix. "But she'll be with Terrock, scouring the land for bad guys. Terrock has a way of easing tensions between small groups or individuals. His powers wouldn't work on Cinder, or his loyalists, but perhaps on small groups of Steam. You see, when a Droplet turns to Steam, it usually takes a few hours for him to totally renounce the goodness that he had as a Droplet. We're hoping that as the battle rages on, Terrock can get some of the new Steam to surrender or even fight for our side."

"I will protect your mother," Terrock promised. "I've found a good spot for your Mom to stay. She'll be a good luck charm for me."

The children were grateful that Mom wouldn't be engaging the enemy directly.

"And you, Dad?" Jack asked.

"I'll be fine Jack," Dad reassured the boy. "King Momo has placed me in one of his finest regiments, and I probably won't even have to do much."

"Exactly how will you fight the Steam?" Brandon asked. "You can't even see them, and if you could, you can't harm gas. The swords will be useless."

"A very bright boy," King Momo interceded. "Droplets are able to see Steam and your parents will be provided with masks, such as yours, so they may see their enemy. And if you've noticed, we're all armed with bellows, so that we can suck the vermin out of existence. The swords are for the Flappers and Mole Rats, or Cinder if we should find him first."

"Speaking of Mole Rats," Volcanius interjected, "you and Jack will likely see some of them as you get closer to Cinder's lair. They're quite ugly. Cinder has placed a spell on these usually non-aggressive creatures, giving them a voracious appetite for intruders. Your swords should serve you well."

Felix provided the boys with a detailed map of the tunnels, two aluminum swords (lighter than steel), and the gas masks.

"Put on the masks when Greely tells you to," Felix instructed. "And leave them on until he tells you it's safe."

Brandon looked at the map and swallowed hard. It was a very detailed map of a very detailed tunnel system. He handed the map to Jack, remembering how well he did at navigating the tunnels to find JayJay.

"Remember to stay on the path," Volcanius warned. "I will be able to speak to you only sporadically throughout your journey, and sometimes in much muted tones. The farther you get from my mouth, the harder it will be for me to communicate with you. And there are numerous dangers that you'll face if you stray from the planned route."

Dad was getting into his battle gear. He wore a metal suit underneath a special cloth material. This material was developed by the Droplet Wise, the thinkers and mages from Zucarus, to protect the wearer from burns. He wore tight fitting gloves of the same material. The metallic under garments would protect from the steel weapons or fangs of their enemies. He also had a mask to wear once he made contact with the Steam, as well as some water and Fruit.

Terrock held Mom in his grasp, a field of wildflowers and grass, and positioned her in front of the boys. She wore a dress of the anti-burn material and had a mask at her disposal. She also had some jugs of water and some Great Fruit to sustain her.

Stepping down from her floral platform, Mom hugged the children until Dad tapped her on the shoulder. Mom and Dad kissed.

"Let's synchronize our watches, Brandon," Dad said. They confirmed that it was now 6:53 - five hours and seven minutes until the beginning of the revolution.

"We love you very much," Mom whispered to Brandon and Jack. Dad nodded. She was trying to be strong, for them. She was unable to utter another word despite wanting to offer advice, as all of her strength was being used to hold back tears.

Terrock whisked Mom away. The simple fragrant breeze left a lasting impression on those that remained.

Dad patted Brandon on the shoulder. Then it was Jack's turn.

No words were spoken.

Dad joined his assigned regiment, a group of very large Droplets. Each soldier was nearly twice Dad's size and they carried huge bellows and either a sword or mace. The image of these combatants comforted Brandon and Jack. They knew that Dad would be in good hands.

General Moist called the entire army to attention and then commanded them to march toward their assigned destination. Most were heading west, to the Steam Soldier's encampment, while about a fifth of them, including Dad, marched north behind Bellock. Their plan was to attack the northern Steam armies, including the elite forces that might try to set up a barricade to protect their evil master.

"Well, here we go," Brandon said to Jack, both dressed in their protective gear.

"Brandon, do you think we'll be able to change the prophecy?" Jack asked. He was understandably nervous.

"Jack, we don't even know all the details around it," Brandon stated. "I'm not sure we'll even know if we're changing anything or not. But as long as we have faith."

"I'm scared," Jack confessed.

"I know," Brandon said. "Me too." He gathered his sword and bellows and put them in a special belt that had been given to him. Jack did the same. He handed his brother the map, recognizing him as the navigator of the group. Then Brandon flung a satchel over his shoulder which contained some water, Great Fruit, matches in case the flashlight died, and some small vials of liquid that he couldn't identify.

"You guys ready?" Brandon asked of Greely and JayJay. The answer was in the affirmative.

They walked to the mouth of the cave.

Brandon tried to think of something profound to say, as unofficial leader of the group. Then he decided that maybe "profound" wouldn't settle his brother's nerves.

He took his younger brother by the shoulders and looked him dead in the eye. He waited a few seconds and then blurted out "Peanut butter gumballs!"

 Jack looked at him curiously. And then, the two of them began a laughing fit that put all their previous ones to shame. There was even laughter coming from their companions.

"What?!?" Jack said finally, trying to catch his breath.

"I don't know," Brandon responded, still giggling. "Maybe it could be our battle cry."

More laughter.

Chapter 14

The tunnels were narrower than expected as the foursome traveled into the depths of Volcanius.

There was still some communication with their host. He would often give them updates on the movement of King Momo's troops and of Terrock's and Bellock's current location. Most of the time, Brandon and Jack just wanted to know that Mom and Dad were o.k.

The heat was getting to them a little bit. Sometimes they'd turn down the wrong path and come face to face with a stream of lava flowing through black rock. It was always a shock, singeing their skin just a little bit. When it happened, JayJay and Greely were motherly in their behavior, furiously flapping their wings in an effort to cool off their young friends.

It was about 10:00 when they met their first true obstacle, a Mole Rat and his pack. JayJay warned his party about their presence, as he and Greely took turns as advance scouts.

"How many are there," Greely asked.

"Six that I can see, but there could be more," JayJay responded. Since Mole Rats were adept at digging through soil and even rocks, he couldn't be sure if there were more in the tunnel walls.

"We can either fight, or try to sneak past them." Greely offered. Since they were blind, they wouldn't be able to see their visitors. But their hearing and sense of smell were very acute.

"With the way Jack smells," Brandon began, "I don't think we'd make it past them."

"Hey!" Jack protested, lifting one arm and sniffing, then the other, to test his brother's assertion.

"O.K.   Maybe we should fight," he conceded.

"We'll fly ahead," Greely said. "and get them going in the other direction so that you two can surprise them from behind."

The boys readied their swords as Greely and JayJay made their way down the tunnel, where the Mole Rats were feverishly chewing on rock and dirt. The boys followed about 10 steps behind them. The head Mole Rat, Philian, sensed JayJay's and Greely's arrival and lifted his nose in the air. The others soon imitated. As the fliers passed overhead, Philian sounded the alert.

"Intruders!" He shouted. "Get them!" The other five Mole Rats shot past Philian through the narrow passageway. With the flashlight's batteries dwindling, the boys could barely make out the hairless forms in front of them. The wrinkled bodies were almost as large as theirs. Wiry whiskers protruded from their sinister snouts and their razor-sharp claws glistened a bit in the faint light. Their incisors were daggers that dangled from their upper jaws and they were getting closer.

Philian remained in the same spot, as the walls around him crumbled like a stale loaf of pumpernickel. As expected, five additional Mole Rats joined their pack – now there were eleven in all.

They ran in the opposite direction from their brethren toward the Lange kids, while Philian remained behind, perhaps out of cowardice or to protect the rear ranks. With swords in hand, the boys braced for the impact.

"Surrender fools," Philian demanded, in a dry, scratchy voice. His minions set up a barricade across the tunnel floor.

The boys were still. Their swords were raised.

"I can see you," Philian, his nose pointing directly between the boys. More appropriately, he could smell them.

"And we can see you," Brandon responded. "You are the ones who must surrender."

Philian laughed and then began climbing the walls, slowly

at first. His pace picked up and he was soon moving in a spiraling pattern, like a drill, away from the boys.

"Stop him!" Jack screamed, remembering his winged friends, and encouraging them to stop the beast before he escaped to warn others. The other Mole Rats rushed the humans.

Brandon stepped forward and lowered his sword in a violent manner. The blade found its mark on one of the Rat's forehead. Jack took a mighty swing at the next Rat in line and struck it in the shoulder. The boys mimicked the form of swordsmen that they saw in the movies, parrying the advances of the giant rodents while thrusting their weapons with great force into the tough flesh of the beasts. They noticed that Greely and JayJay were able to halt Philian's retreat keeping him occupied with alternating aerial attacks.

But their movements quickly changed from that of dashing swashbucklers. The blind creatures found the boys sneakers and pant legs, and began gnawing at them.   Good form quickly turned to frantic actions. Despite the heat and their fatigue, Brandon and Jack maneuvered their weapons in flashy fashion. Together, the blades were like a giant blender, tearing down the ingredients of a Mole Rat shake. Yuck!

The lower level leaches latched onto Brandon's legs, spinning him around. Jack was in no less peril, with three rats climbing and scratching their way up his torso. Philian had given up his attempts at escape and turned his attention to the boys. He lunged for Brandon's chest and began lashing out with his razor-sharp claws as the others remained focused on his legs and feet. Brandon's shirt became a tattered mess, but the protective undergarment protected him from a more unfortunate fate.

Greely and JayJay tried to help as much as they could. The gull was a bit more effective, pecking the faces of the shriveled-up foes. JayJay merely flapped his wings and sang songs, making the scene rather comical to anyone who noticed.

Greely was able to get a few rats off of Jack and soon the boy was free to help his brother.

Jack's swipes were surprisingly precise. He struck several rabid rodents as Brandon struggled with the leader.

Once again, JayJay offered some assistance by doing his little musical dance over the head of Philian.

At that moment, the boys realized that he was attempting to wreak havoc with the rats' senses. Philian began flailing at the air, instead of Brandon's body. The elder Lange pushed the chief rat off of him and tackled him to the ground.

During the melee, Volcanius offered some assistance. Knowing that there was some violent struggle going on within him, he spoke words of encouragement to the boys. His booming voice occasionally distracted the Mole Rats as they tried to listen to the swords' slashing sounds to avoid their aluminum wrath.

The two rolled around on the dirt floor, each trying to avoid their enemy's blows as well as the jagged rocks that littered the ground. With the other foes either badly wounded or dead, Jack's attention was solely on the king rat. A high-pitched squeal rang out through the tunnel and it was at that moment that the Good realized they had vanquished their formidable enemy.

It was over in less than 15 minutes.

"Brandon?" Jack began. His heart was beating through his chest. His hair was matted down from the perspiration and elements that enveloped his head.

"Yeah," Brandon replied, breathing heavily.

"I don't feel well," Jack exclaimed. Brandon handed him a bottle of water and a piece of fruit.

"You need to eat something," Brandon explained. "That's all

it is." He worried that maybe his brother wouldn't be up for the battles that lay ahead. A second grader shouldn't be asked to do such things. It was hard enough for an eleven year old.

"Put on your masks," Greely suggested. "The sulfur vapors may be causing you some discomfort."

The boys complied. Brandon shared a piece of the Great Fruit and a few sips of water. He offered them to JayJay and Greely, but they refused, saying they had eaten and drank plenty prior to their journey.

The masks were more comfortable than they would have guessed, almost like putting a soft, thin baggy over their heads. They were able to breathe better, without the obnoxious odor irritating their noses and throats.

"I meant that I don't feel good about what we just did," Jack explained further. He looked down at his sword as it dangled from his grip, its point poking the dirt ground. He began making designs in the reddish brown floor.

"I know," Brandon responded. After a long pause he continued. "Sometimes we have to do difficult things for the good of ... well Good." He put his arm around Jack and squeezed gently.

"I think I'll be o.k. when we face Cinder, 'cause he's so evil,"

Jack continued. "But these creatures were more like wild animals. They didn't know any better."

"Jack," a thunderous voice sounded. Volcanius interrupted their discussion to give his own opinion on the matter. "Every creature in this world has chosen to be on the side of Good or Evil. They're not like animals from your world. Even those taken from your dimension have been given the gift of knowledge about this world and its evil dictator. While their actions may imitate the ignorant innocents, each creature here is given the option of choosing where they cast their lot."

His voice was barely audible, but the kids got the point.

"It's still hard," Jack argued. "By killing, aren't we becoming that which we're trying to destroy."

"**No**," Volcanius responded. "You are not killers. You are protectors of Good. Your actions are necessary to stop an evil entity from taking over this world and yours. Do not forget *why* you do what you do."

"And if it's not enough," Brandon added, "if it's all in vain?" He wiped his sweaty brow and looked up at the tunnel ceiling, imagining Volcanius' craggy face.

"I don't believe that the fight against evil can ever be in vain," Volcanius responded. "We must never give up the battle for what is right."

Greely and JayJay remained silent. There wasn't much more they could say, to offer solace to the boys for what just occurred.

"I am a mountain," Volcanius said. "I've been around for thousands of years. I've seen good and evil rise and fall. But because we are encased in this strange world, the results of a waged war can have everlasting impact. Evil could destroy all that is good, if we don't rise up against it. And if Evil prevails in Zucarus, it is not known how far Cinder can extend his frightful domain. Will your world be next?"

The cause seemed right. And despite their reservations about how they might find victory, the boys vowed to carry on.

Jack said a quick prayer over the bodies of the Mole Rats. A faint whisper could be heard at the base of one of the walls.

"thank you," it said.   The sound came from one of the Mole Rats, a lone survivor who lay dying.

Jack and Brandon leaned over the fallen rodent, straining to hear the words.

"Thank you," he repeated. They couldn't understand the

words spoken by the weak voice.

"I can't understand you," Brandon said, removing his breathing apparatus. The air was biting. His nostrils burned. He looked at the creature, tears welling in his eyes. Jack placed a hand on the creature's back and removed his own mask with his other hand.

The rodent inhaled deeply, propped himself up on his front legs and mustered his last bit of strength.

"Thank you," he said. *"...finally free."* With that, he collapsed on the ground, his last breath expelled.

Greely and JayJay stood watch and urged the boys to move on. It was getting late and they still had many more yards to navigate.

"You two are truly ambassadors for Good," Greely stated emphatically. "You show remorse for necessary but distasteful actions, and pity for a fallen foe."

"And what good did it do?" Brandon wondered aloud, agreeing to continue the trek. He walked with Jack down the pathway to the next tunnel crossway.

As Greely and JayJay began to follow, they saw the tunnel walls crumbling around them. At least 25 Mole Rats tumbled onto the tunnel floor around them, some in front, and some behind. Greely and JayJay readied themselves for a new fight and prepared to warn the boys.

But before they could utter a single word, the pack called out in unison, "*Finally free!!!*"

The wall dwellers scurried down the tunnel, in the opposite direction, away from the boys. As they disappeared into the darkness, sounds of joy could still be heard.

"What was that?" Brandon asked, after retracing his steps to the site of the recent commotion.

"*That was the sound of extreme gratitude,*" JayJay responded, translated by Greely.

Chapter 15

It was 11:15.   According to Volcanius' last report, the pieces were in place for the assault by King Momo's troops on the western front and the attack in the north by his elite forces. Terrock was busy traveling the kingdom with Mom, inspiring individual Cinder followers to renounce their patronage to the Great Fire Wizard.

It had been a while since the foursome was able to communicate with the Mesa Man. They heard sounds on occasion, which comforted them, but all intelligible conversation was done. The four had agreed to keep their own conversations to a minimum, to avoid detection by Cinder's guards.

"What's that? "Jack asked, pointing to a green mist that he spotted about 40 feet from where the foursome stood.

"What do you see?" Greely asked.

"It looks like some kind of greenish gas," Brandon declared. He was also pointing to the source of emerald air.

"Ahhh," Greely whispered. "It must be the Steam Soldiers."

"But I thought they were invisible," Jack answered, straining his eyes to make out any figures within the gaseous creation.

"King Momo has some magic too, you know," Greely explained. "Your masks allow you to view the Steam Soldiers. That may make things a bit easier for us."

"Cool," Brandon uttered. "I didn't think we were there yet, Cinder's lair, I mean."

"No," Greely replied. "This is only the outer edges of his guards. We're close, but the ESB [elite forces] won't be found until we're just outside of Cinder's chamber."

"But are we supposed to wait here until 12:00 or do we get closer?" Jack asked.

"Oh, I'm guessing we need to get closer," Brandon responded.

Greely nodded.

"*It's bellows time,*" JayJay announced.

The boys put their swords in their sheaths and removed the bellows from their belts. They tested them out a couple of times, allowing the air to fill them up before squeezing it out again. It made a high-pitched whining sound, almost a whistle. They thought their enemy had surely heard these sounds, but there was no movement by the green mist, other than the swirl patterns created in the room up ahead.

"The Steam Soldiers will likely begin to form as we get

closer," Greely explained. "You'll be able to make out individual forms of each soldier."

"Do we blow them away, or suck them in," Jack asked, more than a bit excited.

"That depends," Greely replied. "If they're advancing too quickly, just blow them away, but if you're able to suck them in, just push the button on the side of the device and you'll be able to capture the soldiers and repeat the step over and over. Just remember to push the button, or you'll blow them back out. And don't remove your mask for any reason."

As the group managed their way through the last passage way, the green gas formed into soldiers, similar in size and shape to the Droplet warriors, and proceeded toward the trespassers. They were armed only with sticks that they held in mid-air and rocks that they scraped from the tunnel walls as they approached the good guys.

"Peanut butter gumballs!!" Jack yelled. It seemed to take them all by surprise, friends and foes alike.

Sticks were swung and rocks flew. JayJay and Greely were hit a few times by the projectiles, but it didn't stop their counter-attacks. The green gas managed to slow them down a bit, as its poison worked its way into their lungs. But neither would die from the venomous air, as they had built up immunity from years of living in this crazy land.

The bellows worked wondrously as the kids were having more fun than they should have, sucking up the Steam Soldiers into their tiny prisons. A few cuts and bruises would be a small price to pay for taking out the outlying ranks of Cinder's tunnel army.

Brandon and Jack underestimated the number of soldiers that they had to face, but they were getting better and better at using the bellows. With only a few soldiers left floating around, Brandon got a bit cocky and began teasing his brother.

"Watch out Jack!" Brandon playfully yelled, squirting out a Soldier directly into Jack's face. Brandon sucked it back in before it could get too far.

"Stop it!" Jack yelled, but his laughter betrayed him. Brandon squirted out another one. This time, the end of the bellow got a bit too close to Jack's mask, knocking it ever so slightly and leaving a gap between the material's edge and Jack's neck.

The remaining Steam Soldiers recognized the opening and flew into the open mask like a swarm of vicious bees.

"Jack!" Brandon exclaimed, his eyes wide with terror.

"The bellows Jack, use the bellows quickly!" Greely demanded.

Brandon used his weapon on the green mist that engulfed Jack's face.

"*Hold your breath Jack*," JayJay said.

It took seven or eight attempts to capture the Soldiers who were intent on finding refuge in Jack's nose and mouth. Finally, the last bit of green air slipped into the bellow's nozzle.

"I'm sorry Jack! I'm so sorry!!" Brandon said. He shook his brother slightly, as the younger sibling's eyes began to close. He removed his own mask in anticipation of having to do mouth-to-mouth resuscitation.

"I'm o.k." Jack managed. "It burns, but I think I'm o.k."

Brandon hugged his brother tightly and resumed the apologies.

"Both of you put your masks on, and leave them on," Greely said.

"He's going to be o.k., right?" Brandon asked Greely.

"It's a very toxic poison but hopefully he didn't breath in too much of it," Greely opined. "Take the vial of purple liquid out of your pack."

Brandon complied. He felt sick to his stomach. He knew it was all his fault. He shouldn't have been playing around, especially in such a dangerous place. Sensing the boy's deep regret and his possible surrender to it, Greely offered some hope.

"He didn't lose consciousness and you got the Soldiers out pretty quickly," Greely began. "The liquid is Luxim and should work as an antidote."

Brandon uncorked the small bottle and gave it to Jack.

"Just a small sip. That's all." Greely instructed.

Jack took a sip and smiled. "This isn't bad."

"I'm glad you like minced toad liver," JayJay said. Jack's face went white, but he was grateful that the vial had been included in the satchel.

It was 11:45. They were extremely close to their destination, but the four agreed to take a brief rest.

"I'm so sorry Jack," Brandon said quietly.

"What do you call two kids, a bird, and a butterfly trying to defeat a terrible dragon?" Jack interrupted, trying to change the subject.

"I don't know, what?" Brandon asked.

"Crazy," Jack answered. Soft laughter filled the chamber.

The laughter traveled into the next corridor, and then the next, until it's muffled cadence filled the ears of an awakening black-winged creature named Cinder.

Chapter 16

Resuming their odyssey, the four quickly found the outer chamber leading to Cinder's lair. It was still a good 100 feet away. Between them and a large gold door that surely led into Cinder's room, there were hundreds of Flappers, hovering in space, from floor to ceiling, barely concealing a group of thirty regular and ten ESB guards aligning the walls that directly bordered the door.

Jack was feeling much better now. The boys found a spot in a nearby alcove, where they waited for the hands on Brandon's watch to reach the twelve. There were only four minutes until King Momo's armies would strike.   They hoped that they'd have a rejuvenated youngster to help in their own cause.

Suddenly, the Flappers divided into groups of two and positioned themselves against the walls, facing each other. This provided Greely and the brothers with a perfect view of the ESB guards.

The mask allowed the boys to see them as green soldiers with heavy armor and either spears, axes, or swords. Their gaseous bodies were thick. Red flames sat in the hollows, where their eyes would be. Gaseous striations gave flesh-like form to their long cheeks. There was an aura about them. It would not be so easy to defeat these demons.

Without the special masks Greely and JayJay only saw some floating metal plates and weaponry.

The seconds ticked by. It was 11:59.

Brandon just glanced up from his watch when he heard his brother cry out.

"Peanut butter gumballs!!!!" Jack shouted. They were supposed to wait until 12:00 and sneak into the lair by using stealthy tactics, but the gauntlet had been thrown down. Jack would later tell his brother that he thought he'd try a different approach, in hopes of knocking the prophecy off of its sturdy pedestal.

To the astonishment of the group, the Flapper guards remained at their positions along the walls. Half expecting them to attack as they ran through, Brandon and Jack swatted at imaginary mosquitoes as their swords flailed every which way above their heads. But the Flappers never approached.

Seeing this, JayJay and Greely flew ahead to address the elite guards. But another shocking development surfaced. The ESB guards merely stood aside, presenting the four with access to the gold door.

It was 12:00.

There was no clamoring of guards rushing to the aid of the western and northern regions of Zucarus where King Momo's armies and allies lay siege. What was happening topside? Were the original plans still intact? There was no recent word from Volcanius. Did Jack's decision to start things sooner than planned impact the scheme of the Good's military?

The four approached the golden door. There were no attempts to stop them.

There was no door knob or hinges. What was originally identified as gold was merely a brightly painted wooden door. They stared at it for minutes, as eyes of the ESB and regular guard focused on them.

Before they could decide on their next move, the door swung open with a hissing sound. The wooden door slammed into the cave wall with great force, splintering on impact. A bright orange light shown from within, practically blinding the visitors. They shielded their eyes.

"Welcome," hissed an unseen creature from within. It sounded like Cinder.

Brandon and Jack exchanged looks. Without a word between them, they both took three giant steps and entered the room.

It wasn't a room as much as a vast expanse of space, the size of an indoor football stadium. Hot embers from a recently stoked fire sat in the middle of the room. Lava streams flowed in a spider-web pattern along the rock floor. The ceiling was over a hundred feet high and was adorned by hundreds of glittering stalactites. Around the edges of this coliseum, where the fans would typically sit, stood thousands of Steam Soldiers, uniformly positioned. At the far end of the chamber, barely visible, Cinder sat in dragon form on a large rock ledge, enjoying the shocked expressions on the boys' faces.

Greely and JayJay took their positions on the boys' shoulders, fearful of what was about to come, but remaining loyal to their comrades.

The dragon puffed out his chest and thrust out his wings. He flapped once and rose from his perch. It only took three seconds for him to fly across the arena and settle onto a rock slab situated a few feet from his enemies.

"Welcome, young ones," Cinder began. His voice shook the entire room. Chants of "Cinder" erupted throughout the cavern.

"Think they'll do the wave?" Brandon asked Jack. Jack smiled.

"Silence," Cinder demanded. "I find your humor to be

misplaced. The two of you …"

"Four," Greely corrected, flapping his wings for emphasis.

"Fine. The four of you stand before the Great Fire Wizard, sure to meet a fiery death, and you make jokes?" The dragon peered down, bringing his smoking nostrils closer to the boys' faces. They coughed through their masks as the smoke seemed to penetrate the thin veil. "Now that's funny," Cinder laughed.

"And your parents, and Droplet friends, wasting their efforts in places that have been vacated for the past several day," Cinder continued, "do you find that amusing?"

"What?" Brandon asked, his face turning pale. How did he find out, Brandon wondered? They had been so careful.

Their thoughts turned to their parents. Were they safe?

"Was it a Flapper?" Greely asked, glaring at JayJay as he proudly sat atop Jack's left shoulder. No. He needed no answer. The singing butterfly was a friend. Greely could sense only truth in JayJay's shaking head.

Jack took a step toward Cinder, cocking his head so that he could gaze into the towering beast's eyes. He gritted his teeth and then, in the most serious voice he could muster, he confessed, "It was me."

Chapter 17

"How could you, Jack?" Brandon asked.

"I wanted to protect everyone," Jack explained. "I knew that we could do this on our own and I didn't want to put anyone else in danger, especially Mom and Dad."

"When ...?" Brandon started to ask.

"It was easy," Jack explained. "I saw a Flapper when we were camped out on Volcanius the other night. I told him the basics, and the rest is history. Maybe I changed the prophecy, huh Brandon?"

"And maybe you didn't," Brandon argued. "If all of Cinder's armies are here with us, and Mom and Dad and all of the Droplets are elsewhere, do you really think we stand a chance? Why would Cinder focus all of his attention on us, if he didn't think that our defeat would lead to the fall of Good? "

"I don't know. But evil will fall too," Jack reminded him. "And if we're going to die anyway, I thought maybe we could save Mom and Dad, and the Droplets, so that they can continue the fight against Cinder."

Cinder was enjoying the brotherly feud. Brandon shook his head. With the consequences to their actions fast approaching, he had many doubts about the likelihood of success. But even so, he could see a glimmer of rationality in Jack's plan. It really didn't matter anyway. He wasn't going to use his last breath to yell at his brother.

"O.K.   You win," Brandon said. "What's next?"

"The Challenge," Jack replied.

"Yessssss," hissed Cinder. "The Challenge." Cinder was a believer in the prophecy to a point. But where Brandon and Jack hoped to alter it somehow to avoid their predicted demise, Cinder's ego prevented him from believing that his evil rule would ever come to an end.

"Challenge him! Challenge him Brandon!!" Jack urged. He was jumping up and down now, pointing at Cinder with semi-evil intentions.

"To what?" Brandon asked. "Swords? A fist fight?"

"No, no," Jack responded. "That won't work."

"Then what?" Brandon asked again.

"Tetris!" Jack said with a sly smile.

The Light Box Carrier reached into his back pocket. He turned on his device and noted that the power was at about 15% - probably good enough for a few more games.   His expression transformed from despair to joy in a matter of seconds.

"Yeah," Brandon started. "I challenge you to one game of Tetris. Winner takes all. Winner takes control of this kingdom."

Cinder's expression was unpleasant to say the least. He looked down at the strange device, annoyed that his greatest triumph would come from some "game."

"Wouldn't you prefer swords, or spears?" Cinder asked.

"Nope," Brandon responded.

"Very well," Cinder reluctantly agreed. "You will find defeat in whatever challenge you lay before me. I was just hoping for a more spectacular presentation."

"Oh, well. Here's how the game works," Brandon began, "so pay attention."

"Various colorful shapes, called tiles, will fall from the top of the screen. The object of the game is to maneuver the tiles by pressing the directional arrow buttons so that they fall to the bottom of the screen, eventually creating a complete row. You can also turn the tiles clockwise by hitting this button, to help move the tiles into any empty spaces at the bottom of the screen. If you create a complete row, or multiple rows, they will disappear from the screen and you'll get points.

"But don't leave any gaps in the row or the partial row will remain. With each falling tile, if you fail to create a complete row, you risk having them stack up and reach the top of the screen. If this happens, the game is over. You have to act fast and plan each move."

A glazed look came over Cinder's face.

"Do we get a practice round?" Cinder asked.

"Do you need one?" Jack asked.

"Of course not," Cinder replied.

"I'll go first," Brandon stated confidently, fixing the device in the palm of his hand. "You can watch me to see how it's done."

The blocks fell as the music played. Brandon had done this many times and was quite adept at obtaining high scores. Cinder watched him play, with his chin nearly resting on the boy's left shoulder.

As the points accumulated, Cinder became impatient. He let out a huge sigh that whipped up the air around Brandon's left ear.

"Trying to distract me?" Brandon asked, continuing to rack up points at an amazing rate.

"Not at all," Cinder lied. "I don't need petty tricks to defeat you."

"Get away from him, you big liar!" Jack yelled.

Cinder complied with the request. As he moved away, and turned toward Jack, he wagged his serpent tail. It struck Brandon directly in the back. The handheld game tumbled out of his hands. By the time he picked it up, the last stack of shapes was entering the screen.

'GAME OVER'

"Oops," Cinder uttered.

"You did that on purpose!" Jack yelled.

"It's o.k.," Brandon reassured him, "I just beat my high score."

Jack smiled and turned to Cinder. "Your turn," he said.

Chapter 18

Cinder transformed back into his smaller version. He rolled up the sleeves of his coat, prepared to defeat his young opponent.

"What're you doing?" Brandon asked.

"Preparing to destroy your 'high' score," Cinder said.

"Oh no," Brandon reprimanded, "I didn't challenge *you*."

"Of course you did," Cinder argued. "There are thousands of witnesses who can attest to this fact."

"No," Brandon continued, "I challenged the dragon."

"But the dragon is me," Cinder explained. "We're the same being."

"If you wanted to play in your smaller form, you shouldn't have accepted the challenge in dragon form," Jack challenged.

"What's the difference?" Cinder demanded.

"The difference is, you accepted the challenge as one creature," Brandon said, "and now you want to change things. You either want to accept the challenge or not."

The arena was quieter now. The chants of "Cinder" had

dissipated and the audience was now glued to the verbal exchanges between the combatants.

"If you can't beat him, just say it," Jack insisted.

"I can beat you in any form," Cinder replied. "Here, give me the light box."

Brandon handed the dragon the miniature video game. It nearly got lost in the dragon's large paws.

The boy reset the game and pushed the pause button.

"Any time you're ready," Brandon said. "You just have to push the pause button again, to start the game."

The monstrous dragon stared down at the screen. The box sat in his left hand while an outstretched finger on the other hovered over the gaming system. He had a curious expression on his face. It wasn't quite anger. Brandon had seen it on some of his classmates, just before they first attempted to imitate Brandon's practiced slap-dancing routine.

Cinder tapped the screen with the claw on his right index finger but nothing happened. He tried again, and again the game remained paused.

"What is happening?" He demanded. "Why won't this work?"

"It works fine," Brandon responded. "Do you want me to start the game for you?" He said this loudly so that many Steam Soldiers could hear.

"Nonsense," Cinder said. "I can do it myself." With each subsequent attempt, the dragon resembled a nervous typist trying to get her work done.   'Click-click, clickity-click-click-click'.

Finally, one accidental stroke of his razor-sharp finger nail hit just right. The game started and the music blared. *Doo-de-doo doo, da-da-da, Doo-de-doo do, da da-da*

The crowd resumed their chants. The mouths of the soldiers moved in unison and their song reverberated throughout the arena. Some nearby ESB guards raised their weapons in the air and made some violent pronouncement that was only understood by their own kind.

Brandon and Jack just smiled.

It was pure luck that the dragon managed to un-freeze the game, and now he was desperately trying to use the arrow buttons to maneuver the pieces in place. The colorful shapes were raining down the screen, mocking Cinder's attempts to get them aligned in some sort of pattern.

Doo-de-doo doo, da-da-da, Doo-de-doo do, da da-da

"Wait," Cinder stammered. The shapes fell and the color of each was reflected in the dragon's bowling ball sized eyes.

Another accidental tap flipped one of the green shapes, spinning it clockwise forty-five degrees. It continued to make its way to the bottom of the screen.

Doo-de-doo doo, da-da-da, Doo-de-doo do, da da-da

Click-click-click-click

Nothing happened. The dragon began breathing heavily. His fingers moved quickly but ineffectively over the Tetris screen. There soon were fifteen tiles clogging up the bottom of the screen, showing lots of gaps between them so as not to allow the formation of a single clean row.

Doo-de-doo doo, da-da-da, Doo-de-doo doo, da da-da

Click-click-clickity-click-click-click

Five more tiles fell. Then five more. The stack of shapes was nearly reaching the top of the screen. The dragon put the game in the other hand and attempted to push buttons with the other. It was no use.

Click-click-clickity-click-click-clickity

Two more tiles and the tiles would reach the top. Sensing defeat, the Dragon reared back on its hind quarters and threw the game into the crowd.

Doo-de-doo doo, da-da-da, Doo-de-doo do, da da-da

"Here it is," a Steam Soldier announced, picking up the game and offering it back to the Great Fire Wizard.

Wah-wah-wah – Clack

"Game over," Brandon mused.

Flames came out of Cinder's nose and mouth. His eyes rolled back into their sockets and a low growl grew.

"NooooooooOOOOOOOOO!!!" screamed the vanquished gamer.

"Take that!" Jack yelled, poking his sword into the scaly hide of the beast. He continued to thrust his weapon into the impenetrable side, mocking him gleefully. Each jab represented a recent bad memory that he was trying to exterminate. Like most bullies, Cinder merely cowered under his veil of false bravado. He looked around the great arena for support, his eyes darting here and there, but found none. His anger turned to blind fury and finally to a kind of craziness that typically precedes an unexpected action.

"That enough," Brandon commanded, resting a hand on his brother's left shoulder. The youngster had expended most of his energy and was breathing hard. "He can't hurt us anymore."

With two flaps of his mighty wings, he was twenty-five feet off of the ground. Then with one mountain-shaking flap, his body became a hulking missile that soared up to through the ceiling of the Great Arena.

Smoke poured out through the hole behind him as Cinder continued his ascent.

The crowd was left silent, gazing up through the dark vertical tunnel. The dragon could no longer be seen. Several seconds passed before a crashing sound emanated from the hole. A beam of light shined down through the opening, as randomly sized rock fragments rained down onto the battlefield.

"Grab hold to the satchel!" Greely yelled. A corner of the backpack dangled from the corner of his beak. JayJay hovered next to him. This wasn't part of the plan, but neither was Cinder's sudden lift-off. The satchel was too high for Jack to reach, so Brandon boosted him up. Then, with one hand, he held on as tightly as he could to the bottom of the sack.

Greely strained to lift the boys, his small but muscular body slowing rising, attempting to simulate Cinder's flight pattern. The boys dropped their bellows and swords to lighten the load.

"Fly Greely!!" Brandon shouted, looking down at the scene below. They were just inside the hole in the ceiling but they could see chaos below. ESB, and regular soldiers alike, didn't know what to do. Some tried to follow the fearsome four, but got swept away by the wind currents left in Greely's wake.

The bird climbed and climbed through the hole left by Cinder's departure.

This wasn't what they anticipated. Brandon thought that maybe Cinder would turn into dust as his ego was crushed by the embarrassing defeat. Jack believed that his soldiers might defect and join the side of good.

As they approached the apex of their flight, essentially the top of Volcanius' head, they could see the golden light from the Zucarus sky. It framed Cinder perfectly as he became a tiny dot, a meaningless mass, in the evening sky.

Greely let Brandon and Jack drop to a nearby ledge. Then he and JayJay joined them, all exhausted.

A thunderous boom echoed throughout the land, followed by a lightning flash of yellow. Then, there was no golden sky – only darkness. The boys could barely see each other as they sat no more than four feet from each other on the rock balcony.

Cinder had flown into his own transparent creation, destroying the barrier that once separated two worlds. No one would know the motivations behind Cinder's ballistic path. Was he trying, in one last ditch effort, to expand his evil dominion? Or less likely, was he giving the gift of escape to his triumphant foe? In any case, the dragon would never know the consequences of his actions, as his pulverized and near lifeless body hovered above his once mighty kingdom.

Chapter 19

Volcanius mumbled, but could not speak. Cinder had ripped through his voice box when he bored through the mountain to reach the surface. If he could have spoken, he would have warned the four about the incoming carcass.   He shook himself to get their attention.

"Gee whiz, Volcanius," Jack said, "can you stop moving around so much? We're tired."

Volcanius shook more.

Brandon, now lying on his back, watched the night sky, a sky similar to the one he remembered from back home.

"Hey!" he exclaimed. "The roof is gone!!" He pointed skyward, finally realizing it.

"He must have rammed into the golden sky," Greely said referring to Cinder's flight path.

"Is that him?!?" Jack asked, pointing to a dark blot in the sky that seemed to be growing as seconds ticked off of Brandon's watch.

"Evil will fall," Brandon remembered. Cinder's body fell fast and the dark shadow became more as the boys could now make out the dragon's ghastly silhouette. It seemed to be coming straight for them.

SCREEEEEEEEEEEEEEEEEEEEEEEEE came an obnoxiously ear-splitting cry from above. Cinder's body was limp but the sound that came out was alive with revenge. The Mesa Man shook again and then snatched up the ledge-dwellers and propelled them out into space, on his extended left arm, to a spot far from Cinder's intended landing spot.

Gaseous forms sprouted from Volcanius' mouth and from the hole left by Cinder. Hundreds of his minions had made it to the surface and many more followed. With his last gasp of legendary breath, Cinder was calling forth his army for a final stand against Good.

THOOOOM

The body fell onto the mountainside, in a heap that surely would have killed Brandon, Jack and their flying buddies. It left a large crevice just below Volcanius' chin. The black dragon was no more, but as the Steam Soldiers exited the mountain, some of them passed through Cinder's lifeless body, temporarily re-animating him as a twitching marionette.

The mountainside was soon overrun by Steam Soldiers. They advanced on the earthen platform that was Volcanius' left arm. They were hot with rage.

The boys looked around for support. In the distance they could see Terrock in the south, with what seemed like a brigade of Droplets flanking him. In the north, Bellock and more armies of Droplets, no doubt including Dad, slowly marched toward Volcanius' position. While the boys were comforted to some extent by the belief that their parents were safe amongst their allies, they also knew that they were too far away to offer any real support. And even if they could reach them in time, the divisions of Evil would outnumber the battalions of Good a thousand to one.

The Steam Soldiers were within a hundred feet of the boys. It was too much for Volcanius to take. He knew he had to do something, but what? From the depths of his lava-filled heart, the Mesa Man's fury fueled a metamorphosis. The massive mountain rumbled and quaked. Gray smoke billowed from his pores. The heat on the mountainside rose instantly by twenty degrees. Soon, bright orange gobs of molten rock colored the landscape like the paintbrush strokes of an experienced artist. The dark night was interrupted by shooting lava stars and a display of magmatic fireworks.

Volcanius covered the four with is a cupped right hand, to protect them from the manifestations of his temper.

Brandon's watch glowed green in their rock cocoon. They'd be protected, at least temporarily, but what of their parents and the Droplets.

"Volcanius!" Brandon yelled. "Let us out!!" He repeated his pleas and asked Jack to join him.

When the mountain finally released them from their cage, the valley was covered with a thick layer of steam. The armies of Droplets were gone, replaced by newly formed Steam Soldiers.   Jack began to cry. Their large friend, in his attempts to save them, transformed their allies into enemies. Neither he nor Brandon knew what had become of Mom and Dad.

"And Good will fall," Brandon muttered.

The Steam Soldiers were almost upon them. Needless reinforcements littered the valley, only highlighting the hopelessness of the moment.

The boys still had their masks on so they could plainly see the hatred in the eyes of the advancing horde.

"Look for a weapon," Brandon ordered.

Jack picked up a few rocks. Greely found a large tree limb, its end still glowing from the earthen fire that had fallen upon it minutes earlier.

Volcanius used his empty hand to swat at the Steam Soldiers and ESB as they approached the four.

His massive mitt worked well to blow many of the soldiers

off of the platform that had become the four's temporary sanctuary. Unfortunately, they'd quickly re-form and begin their ascent anew.

Greely and JayJay vigorously flapped their wings, allowing some room between Brandon and Jack and the Steam army. They had to be tired, but desperation and love for the boys proved to be their unending supply of fuel.

Brandon and Jack, with their backs to each other, fought with tree limb and rocks, respectively, holding back the poisonous gas warriors for as long as they could.

"The vials!" Brandon exclaimed. "Take them out Jack."

Jack reached into the satchel at his feet. He removed three vials and uncorked them all.

"What now?" Jack asked.

"We all take sips and spit it at them," Brandon said, not knowing if his plan would work. He hoped it would somehow defeat the green goblins, or at the least protect them from the poison gases that now seemed to be seeping under their masks. Perspiration and extended wear caused the straps of the masks to expand, no longer providing a perfect protective seal.

They did as Brandon suggested. The kids lifted their masks

and took a swig or two. Then they filled their mouths with the elixir and spat it out at the unsuspecting Steam soldiers. They repositioned the masks on their heads because although they no longer needed them to protect them from the poison, they still allowed them to see the incoming enemy. They repeated the process numerous times until the vials of magenta liquid was gone.

Brandon started to drink the dark pink liquid from the remaining vial. He wasn't sure what would happen but he wanted to spare Jack any negative side effects in case it wasn't meant for human consumption.

"Stop," Greely said. "Only The Speaker should drink that. Its effects can only be felt by him."

Brandon handed Jack the vial. The Speaker chugged the pink liquid but nothing seemed to happen.

While their armor protected them from most of the heavy weaponry being cast their way, the suffocating fog rolled over them.

Tears flowed freely from both boys as they reluctantly abandoned their offensive actions and held each other in a bear hug that even the most elite ESB soldier couldn't break.

"I'm sorry," Jack said. "This is all my fault."

"Nonsense," Brandon insisted, "we wouldn't have lived this long if it hadn't been for you."

"I love you, Brandon," Jack declared.

"I love you too, Jack," Brandon replied.

Greely and JayJay hadn't given up but fatigue had surely set in.

"Thanks for your help and friendship, Greely. And yours too JayJay." Brandon stated, still hugging his brother tightly, but starting his good-byes.

Chapter 20

Unbeknownst to them, as their tears merged and fell to the rocky soil, a single drop chose a different path. Into the dark sky, the shimmering tear rose.

"Good-bye Mom and Dad," Brandon cried out, knowing that neither would hear him.

"I wish they were with us," Jack added.

"They are." Brandon promised.   "And we'll all be to*gether*..." Brandon paused as a cool drop fell onto his hand. He stepped back from his brother and looked at his smudged face. How did Jack's tear or his own for that matter, reach a hand that firmly rested on his brother's back.

"Think of a riddle," Jack asked, confused by his brother's expression. Brandon felt another cool drop on the top of his nose and he knew that his brother was not the cause of this one. "Please," Jack begged.

"Yeah, sure," Brandon said. He thought for a moment and then continued, "What comes down but never goes up?"

"What?" Jack asked, wiping away a tear that neither he nor his brother had shed, and then another.

"Rain," Brandon replied. He smiled widely but this time his

brother didn't share his sense of ill-timed humor.

Another cool drop, and then another, landed between the siblings.

"Huh?" Jack mumbled. "That's not one of your better ones."

"But it will be," Brandon countered.

Brandon lifted Jack's chin up as far as he could. The younger boy squinted as drops of water pelted his face.

"Rain," Jack said. He smiled.

"Good will fall," Brandon repeated. He cocked his head back and looked deep into the nighttime sky. The rain got heavier and made tiny splashing sounds upon his cheeks. It was a welcome sound. He opened his mouth as the green mist around the boys seemed to clear a bit.

When they looked down at the puddles that were accumulating at their feet, the boys were met with a sight that would signify the beginning of a *new* end. A rainy day at the beach is not so much fun, but in Zucarus... the boys became giddy with excitement.

Tiny wet soldiers, of more modern form, were being created as the torrential downpour soaked the environment. The minute battlers grew in size until they were head and shoulders above the ESB. Armed with bazooka-like weapons, rocket launchers and water-balloon grenades, they took their orders from an unseen cloud overhead.

"Water in the hole," one shouted. A gigantic splash of liquid caught Brandon and Jack by surprise. But they didn't care. Their laughter was interrupted only briefly as they had to spit out some clear sparkling water that had landed on their tongues from a haphazardly thrown water bomb.

"Let's re-take this hill, men!" another rain man shouted. As the rain fell, the new Droplet troops moved in a coordinated effort throughout Volcanius' massive interior and the valleys below. Sometimes this new force moved as a group of individuals and at other times as a combined force.

Waves splashed across Volcanius's belly and eradicated the fleeing Steam Soldiers who sought refuge in the Mesa Man's belly button. Other waves eradicated ESB elites as they made a last ditch effort to destroy The Speaker and Light Box Carrier.

In the distance, Jack could see Terrock inching closer to their position, with a hand raised in triumph, seemingly not empty.

Mom?

Bellock on the northern front, lumbered toward their position, with what seemed like a human soldier hoisted on his shoulder.

Dad?

"This reminds me of Wildwood," Brandon said.   "All the waves!!"

The Steam Soldiers and ESB were swept up and vanquished, one by one, by the hardy new branch of the Droplet military.

Things were looking up, for all those who were friends with those that were raining down.

Volcanius' voice returned as the rain cooled the lava within him and restored the voice box that had been damaged by the long gone Dragon Wizard.

"Glad to have you back, Volcanius!" Jack said gleefully.

"My voice left me, but I was always with you Jack," Volcanius responded.

"We know," Jack said.

But the more touching reunion came minutes later when the southern and northern Mesa Men returned their human riders to their offspring.

"Brandon! Jack!" Mom exclaimed as she jumped nearly twenty feet down from the grassy ledge that Terrock was extending toward her children.

"Mom!!" Brandon and Jack cried in unison. They caught Mom in a strong embrace as her momentum was carrying her right into their arms.

"Dad!" Jack called.

Dad limped down the side of Bellock's cliff-like arm. He was slightly injured in an ESB attack, but his delight in seeing his family brought him back to near perfect health instantly.

The Original Four hugged for many minutes and reassured each other that each was alright.

"You did it guys," Dad said, putting his arms on his sons' shoulders. "We've won!"

"We knew you could do it," Mom indicated. "We never doubted you."

"We had a lot of help," Brandon submitted, looking at Greely and JayJay, who were both well drenched but ecstatic over the turn of events. Jack patted the ground and smiled up at Volcanius.

Mom and Dad looked at their sons with a mix of pride and

sorrow. The grade schoolers' faces were dirty and marked from the recent battles and trials that they endured. They seemed older somehow. Behind their smiles, Mom and Dad sensed a pain that went deeper than the obvious bumps and bruises that come with a physical struggle. They hoped that their children's emotional injuries could be healed in time by love and a large dose of normalcy.

King Momo appeared behind a line of modern Droplets.

"You did it," the King said, summoning some familiar faces to pay their respects to the victorious lads.

"Your heroism will not long be forgotten," General Moist declared.

"We're very proud of you," Felix said softly. "We're all so very proud, and grateful." The boys ran to give Felix a hug. They squeezed him so hard that he nearly disappeared for a second, reappearing unharmed behind them.

"Our new kingdom is at your service," King Momo said, instructing all those around him to kneel before the Langes. They quickly and willingly complied. "You are world savers, and our new leaders." Then the King dropped down to one knee and bowed sincerely.

"We just want to go home," Jack stated. Mom and Dad quickly agreed, nodding their consent to the lads first order as co-King of Zucarus.

"We appreciate you all, and all that you have done, to save us," Brandon added, "but our home is in our own world. As beautiful as it is here now, we miss our home."

"Besides," Jack interjected, "You'll always be the king here." He motioned for King Momo to rise.

As the four and King Momo's court began making preparations for the Lange's return to their world, the new Droplet armies were busy reconstructing the face of a kingdom and repairing the damage caused by Cinder and his Evil followers.

Chapter 21

The plan was well thought out, but not finalized. No one could come up with a way for the Langes to make it all the way up to the now star-filled sky above.

Greely might be able to carry the boys, individually, but the weight of their parents would be too much for him and the several other birds that inhabited Zucarus. Flappers weren't the answer, as they were much weaker than the gull.

A decision was made to create a Mesa Man pyramid, to get the Langes as close to the sky as possible. Unfortunately, Volcanius couldn't be used as the base, because although powerful, his body (made mostly of hardened lava) would not be able to withstand the weight of both Bellock and Terrock. And because his legs were forever merged with the Zucarus earth, the thought was he could only be an interested observer.

After numerous goodbyes and the rise of an actual sun in the distant blue sky, two Mesa Men began arrangements for the extraction of their human friends. Terrock, leaving the comfy confines of the Zucarus soil began his ascent on the back of his brother. Bellock was easily able to support his sibling and only showed signs of discomfort when Terrock miscalculated a step and landed a foot in big brother's kidney.

Everyone in Zucarus stopped to watch the Cirque du SoStrange performance. Jack wondered how much money he could raise for his school if he sold tickets to this extravaganza. Droplets and humans applauded as Terrock reached Bellock's summit and stood tall upon his shoulders to provide maximum height.

It was quite an unprecedented scene. Imagine a lush tropical mountain, adorned with colorful vegetation and undulating edges, sitting atop a craggily, boulder-faced monolith. Terrock stretched out to determine how close he could get the Lange's to their intended destination.

"Maybe the tow truck will be able to drop a line to us," Mom said with a grin.

"Haven't checked my messages lately. I'm sure they're still on their way." Dad joked.

"What if Terrock tosses us?" Brandon asked.

"It's doubtful," Felix said. "Even with a good throw."

"And if Greely and all of the Flappers blow us the rest of the way?" Brandon offered.

"Could make for a softer landing if they directed their wings properly," General Moist remarked.

"But we can't take a chance that Terrock's throw won't land them short," King Momo determined.

"I'll toss them," Volcanius stated.

"Not from here, you won't," Dad responded.

"No, not from here," Volcanius answered.

The eldest and most powerful Mesa Man began to move at his base. A grimace on his face prompted on-lookers to inquire about his well-being. The mountain was silent but still strained to accomplish some unknown feat.

"What's going on Volcanius?" Brandon asked.

There was no response. The earth shook violently and so did the stack of Mesa Men that were positioned to Volcanius' left.

"Hey, quit the shaking, brother," Bellock urged. "You're gonna topple us."

"Yeah, I'm feeling a bit of nausea," Terrock confirmed.

"That's all we need, mountain throw-up," Brandon mused. Jack laughed.

"Arrrrrrgh!" Volcanius roared. The mountain tumbled forward, nearly missing the keen observers who gathered to watch. He braced himself with his massive limbs but couldn't halt the momentum and he fell flat on his face. The crowd let out a gasp.

The mighty Mesa Man had ripped himself from the earth, his lower legs still trapped by the stubborn Zucarus soil beneath. He propped himself up on one elbow and grasped a chunk of land with the other. Volcanius pulled himself to the site of the balancing duo.

"What did you do?!?" Jack screamed.

"Merely freed myself so that I can assist in freeing you," Volcanius answered.

The valley was soon filled with thousands of grateful supporters who recognized his giant sacrifice – one that seemed larger than the mountain himself. The Langes didn't know what to say but each silently thanked their friend in their own way.

"Make way for Volcanius!" a Droplet soldier ordered, ushering aside some stragglers who attempted to get a better view.

"Hold steady, brothers," Volcanius instructed as he reached Bellock's right leg. "Stand fast."

Volcanius no longer needed his legs. With powerful arms he

pulled himself up Bellock's legs, then back, until he reached his shoulders, now crowded by the feet of Terrock. The rock ledges and shards of bare minerals scraped Volcanius' torso, but he continued his climb.

After reaching Terrock's legs, he knew that the rest of the journey would be less harsh. In fact, the ferns, bushes, and moss-covered trees tickled his face as he gathered the last bit of strength to scale Terrock's back to sit comfortably on his rounded shoulders.

Bellock strained with the added weight but issued no complaints.

"Well done Volcanius," Terrock commented. Thunderous applause from below convinced Volcanius that he had done the right thing and hope was alive again.

Bellock grabbed the Langes and cradled them in his firm hand and hoisted them above his head to the next transport. The Langes looked down and offered last good-byes to their closest allies – King Momo, General Moist, and of course Felix.

"Goodbye Langes," Bellock said. "Thank you Mr. Speaker and Light Box Carrier! And thank you, Dad. You were a good soldier."

Goodbye Bellock. Thank you.

Terrock's green hand was awaiting them as they reached the higher altitude. They made their connecting flight with time to spare.

Terrock whispered his goodbyes and complimented Mom on her courage and strength. "Your presence allowed us to maintain hope. Thank you all!"

Goodbye Terrock. Thank you.

The last handoff was made. The Langes sat in the palm of Volcanius' right hand, a place made more comfortable due to the greens and flowers that he had collected from Terrock's back as he made his way to his current location.

They looked at Volcanius but couldn't find the words to explain how they felt about their favorite Zucarus landmark – until a young boy spoke.

"We love you Volcanius," Jack said softly. "You've been with us through all of this..."

"Like a rock," Brandon interrupted. He got an elbow from his brother.

"We'll never forget you and what you did for us," Jack continued.

Greely and JayJay had accompanied the Langes on their trip up the mountains. And now, other Flappers arrived on sight to offer their songs, as tributes to those who saved them from their former lives under Cinder's evil reign.

Volcanius couldn't speak. He'd open his mouth but nothing would come out. His voice box worked fine. He couldn't understand why the words just wouldn't come.

"If you break me, I still work," Brandon said. "You can unlock me with an imaginary key. Though I need it, I will freely give it away."

Volcanius tilted his head to the side, like a curious puppy dog.

"What am I?" Brandon asked.

A gentle mountain stream maneuvered down Volcanius' face, like a flowing tear. He looked at Brandon and Jack. He had learned a lot from their visit to Zucarus and would miss them dearly. He understood.

"A heart," Volcanius replied. His back stiffened and he pulled his right arm back.

"And you'll always have ours," Brandon said.

The winds were cool, but refreshing. As Volcanius' arm swung forward, the Langes were propelled through the bright expanse of sky that led to their home world. Flappers flew amongst them, keeping their trajectory true. The songsters would also insure a gentler landing for their friends as they helped to create more amiable air currents.

"Good bye friends," Greely squawked. "Thank you!"

Goodbye Greely. Thank you.

The bird accompanied them on their flight until he reached the invisible barrier that separated two worlds.

With a burst of light and the warmth of a dessert sun, the Nevada locale greeted the Langes as best it could. A strong wind blew a dusting of sand above their heads. The particles swirled and landed on a transparent patch of dessert that was soon covered by a fine layer of beach that hid recent history.

Chapter 22

The car was in the same spot but there weren't any signs that it had been previously buried.

The family trudged several yards to its location and noticed that all four tires appeared to be in working order.   Did AAA come while they were gone?

"Hmmm, that's strange," Dad suggested.

Mom and the boys laughed. Yeah, *that* was strange.

They entered the vehicle.

Dad placed the key in the ignition while the others looked on. The car started almost immediately and the once covered pavement reappeared as if it were directing the Langes to continue on their way.

As Dad drove toward their initial destination, the Sunrise Motel in Ely, not a word was said about their latest adventure. Mom took out her cookbook and began perusing the pages dealing with appetizers. She planned to make a big feast for her family when they returned home and wanted to create a special starter.

Brandon rolled his window down about half way, enjoying the warm breeze on his face. He resumed playing games on his DS, which was surprisingly showing battery life at 75%.

He opted for a super hero battle game rather than Tetris.

Jack found a couple of water bottles under the front seat. They weren't warm, as he figured they would be after time in the dessert heat. He shared some with Mom and Dad but Brandon was too busy to bother. Jack, ever the scavenger, was also able to find some cheese crackers to munch on.

As daytime turned to early evening, the Langes spotted a sign on the edge of the road. It read: Ely 15 miles.

"Looks like we're almost there," Dad said.

Mom put her cookbook down and rested a hand on Dad's arm. "Finally," she replied. "Close the window back there, Brandon."

Brandon either ignored her, or hadn't heard her request. His attention was still focused on the video game and the evil villains who were trying to take him down.   Mom didn't push it. She was in no mood to argue.

"Agent Cheezer stumbles upon a sinister plot involving his Great Nemesis, Meelo the Maniac," Jack murmured.

"What honey?" Mom asked, turning her head slightly so that she could see what the kids were doing. Brandon was still immersed in his video game while Jack was busy putting cracker crumbs into a mostly empty water bottle.

"Jack!" Mom hollered. Dad shifted his eyes to the rear-view mirror.

"What?" Jack asked innocently, as Dad almost drove the car into a nearby ditch.

The car was entering the limits of Ely and the lights from various local establishments were lit, offering a clear path to the Sunrise Motel barely two blocks away.

Without looking up, Brandon reached across the back seat and snatched the water bottle from his brother. He tossed it out the window.

"And everyone lived happily ever after," Brandon said firmly, punching his brother in the arm. Jack knew he deserved that one.

Epilogue:

The water bottled rolled into a gutter in front of the Happy Garden restaurant, its contents saved by a few lucky bounces. A passing stray cat examined the find in hopes of acquiring a morsel or two for dinner. As the feline sniffed the container, a concoction of cool night breeze and warm air from the bottle's interior created a curious fog.

An unsettling sound emanated from *inside* the bottle, as the Langes recuperated in their motel room about a block away.

"*Meowww!*"

20656355R00094

Made in the USA
Middletown, DE
03 June 2015